ALSO BY DEBORAH EISENBERG

Pastorale

Transactions in a Foreign Currency

Under the 82nd Airborne

Air: 24 Hours: Jennifer Bartlett

The Stories (So Far) of Deborah Eisenberg

All Around Atlantis

TWILIGHT OF THE SUPERHEROES

TWILIGHT OF THE SUPERHEROES

DEBORAH EISENBERG

FARRAR, STRAUS AND GIROUX

NEW YORK

Farrar, Straus and Giroux
19 Union Square West, New York 10003

Copyright © 2006 by Deborah Eisenberg
Distributed in Canada by Douglas & McIntyre Ltd.
Printed in the United States of America
First edition, 2006

Grateful acknowledgment is made to the following publications, in which these
stories originally appeared: "Twilight of the Superheroes" in *Final Edition*; "Some
Other, Better Otto" in *The Yale Review*; "Like It or Not" in *The Threepenny Review*; "Window" and "Revenge of the Dinosaurs" in *Tin House*; and "The Flaw in
the Design" in *The Virginia Quarterly Review*.

Library of Congress Cataloging-in-Publication Data
Eisenberg, Deborah.
    Twilight of the superheroes / Deborah Eisenberg.— 1st ed.
        p.   cm.
    Contents: Twilight of the superheroes—Some other, better Otto—
Like it or not—Window—Revenge of the dinosaurs—The flaw in
the design.
    ISBN-13: 978-0-374-29941-5 (alk. paper)
    ISBN-10: 0-374-29941-2 (alk. paper)
    1. New York (N.Y.)—Social life and customs—Fiction.   I. Title.

PS3555.I793T87 2006
813'.54—dc22

                                                                    2005042659

Designed by Jonathan D. Lippincott

www.fsgbooks.com

5   7   9   10   8   6   4

For my darling Wall

CONTENTS

TWILIGHT OF THE SUPERHEROES

The grandchildren approach.

Nathaniel can make them out dimly in the shadows. When it's time, he'll tell them about the miracle.

It was the dawn of the new millennium, he'll say. *I was living in the Midwest back then, but my friends from college persuaded me to come to New York.*

I arrived a few days ahead of the amazing occasion, and all over the city there was an atmosphere of feverish anticipation. The year two thousand! The new millennium! Some people thought it was sure to be the end of the world. Others thought we were at the threshold of something completely new and better. The tabloids carried wild predictions from celebrity clairvoyants, and even people who scoffed and said that the date was an arbitrary and meaningless one were secretly agitated. In short, we were suddenly aware of ourselves standing there, staring at the future blindfolded.

I suppose, looking back on it, that all the commotion seems comical and ridiculous. And perhaps you're thinking that we churned it up to entertain ourselves because we were bored or because our lives felt too easy—trivial and mundane. But consider: ceremonial occasions, even purely personal ones like birthdays or anniversaries, remind us that the world is full of terrifying surprises and no one knows what even the very next second will bring!

Well, shortly before the momentous day, a strange news item appeared: experts were saying that a little mistake had been made—just one tiny mistake, a little detail in the way computers everywhere had been programmed. But the consequences of this detail, the experts said, were potentially disastrous; tiny as it was, the detail might affect everybody, and in a very big way!

You see, if history has anything to teach us, it's that—despite all our efforts, despite our best (or worst) intentions, despite our touchingly indestructible faith in our own foresight—we poor humans cannot actually think ahead; there are just too many variables. And so, when it comes down to it, it always turns out that no one is in charge of the things that really matter.

It must be hard for you to imagine—it's even hard for me to remember—but people hadn't been using computers for very long. As far as I know, my mother (your great-grandmother) never even touched one! And no one had thought to inform the computers that one day the universe would pass from the years of the one thousands into the years of the two thousands. So the machines, as these experts suddenly realized, were not equipped to understand that at the conclusion of 1999 time would not start over from 1900, time would keep going.

People all over America—all over the world!—began to speak of "a crisis of major proportions" (which was a phrase we used to use back then). Because, all the routine operations that we'd so blithely delegated to computers, the operations we all took for granted and depended on—how would they proceed?

Might one be fatally trapped in an elevator? Would we have to huddle together for warmth and scrabble frantically through our pockets for a pack of fancy restaurant matches so we could set our stacks of old New York Reviews ablaze? Would all the food rot in heaps out there on the highways, leaving us to pounce on fat old street rats and grill them over the flames? What was going to happen to our bank accounts—would they vaporize? And what about air traffic control? On December 31 when the second hand moved from 11:59:59 to midnight, would all the airplanes in the sky collide?

Everyone was thinking of more and more alarming possibilities. Some people committed their last night on this earth to partying, and others rushed around buying freeze-dried provisions and cases of water and flashlights and radios and heavy blankets in the event that the disastrous problem might somehow eventually be solved.

And then, as the clock ticked its way through the enormous gatherings in celebration of the era that was due to begin in a matter of hours, then minutes, then seconds, we waited to learn the terrible consequences of the tiny oversight. Khartoum, Budapest, Paris—we watched on television, our hearts fluttering, as midnight, first just a tiny speck in the east, unfurled gently, darkening the sky and moving toward us over the globe.

But the amazing thing, Nathaniel will tell his grandchildren, *was that nothing happened! We held our breath . . . And there was nothing! It was a miracle. Over the face of the earth, from east to west and back again, nothing catastrophic happened at all.*

Oh, well. Frankly, by the time he or any of his friends get around to producing a grandchild (or even a child, come to think of it) they might well have to explain what computers had been. And freeze-dried food. And celebrity clairvoyants and airplanes and New York and America and even cities, and heaven only knows what.

FROGBOIL

Lucien watches absently as his assistant, Sharmila, prepares to close up the gallery for the evening; something keeps tugging at his attention . . .

Oh, yes. It's the phrase Yoshi Matsumoto used this morning when he called from Tokyo. *Back to normal . . . Back to normal . . .*

What's that famous, revolting, sadistic experiment? Something like, you drop the frog into a pot of boiling water and it jumps out. But if you drop it into a pot of cold water and slowly bring the water to a boil, the frog stays put and gets boiled.

Itami Systems is reopening its New York branch, was what Matsumoto called to tell Lucien; he'll be returning to the city soon. Lucien pictured his old friend's mournful, ironic expression as he added, "They tell me they're 'exploring additional avenues of development now that New York is back to normal.' "

Lucien had made an inadvertent squawklike sound. He shook his head, then he shook his head again.

"Hello?" Matsumoto said.

"I'm here," Lucien said. "Well, it'll be good to see you again. But steel yourself for a wait at customs; they're fingerprinting."

VIEW

Mr. Matsumoto's loft is a jungle of big rubbery trees, under which crouch sleek items of chrome and leather. Spindly electronic devices blink or warble amid the foliage, and here and there one comes upon an immense flat-screen TV—the first of their kind that Nathaniel ever handled.

Nathaniel and his friends have been subletting—thanks, obviously, to Uncle Lucien—for a ridiculously minimal rent and on Mr. Matsumoto's highly tolerable conditions of cat-sitting and general upkeep. Nathaniel and Lyle and Amity and Madison each have something like an actual bedroom, and there are three whole bathrooms, one equipped with a Jacuzzi. The kitchen, stone and steel, has cupboards bigger than most of their friends' apartments. Art—important, soon to be important, or very recently important, most of which was acquired from Uncle Lucien—hangs on the walls.

And the terrace! One has only to open the magic sliding panel to find oneself halfway to heaven. On the evening, over three years ago, when Uncle Lucien completed the arrangements for Nathaniel to sublet and showed him the place, Nathaniel stepped out onto the terrace and tears shot right up into his eyes.

There was that unearthly palace, the Chrysler Building! There was the Empire State Building, like a brilliant violet hologram! There were the vast, twinkling prairies of Brooklyn and New Jersey! And best of all, Nathaniel could make out the Statue of Liberty holding her torch aloft, as she had held it for each of his parents when they arrived as children from across the ocean—terrified, filthy, and hungry—to safety.

Stars glimmered nearby; towers and spires, glowing emerald, topaz, ruby, sapphire, soared below. The avenues and bridges slung a trembling net of light across the rivers, over the buildings. Everything was spangled and dancing; the little boats glittered. The lights floated up and up like bubbles.

Back when Nathaniel moved into Mr. Matsumoto's loft, shortly after his millennial arrival in New York, sitting out on the terrace had been like looking down over the rim into a gigantic glass of champagne.

UNCLE LUCIEN'S WORDS OF REASSURANCE

So, Matsumoto is returning. And Lucien has called Nathaniel, the nephew of his adored late wife, Charlie, to break the news.

Well, of course it's hardly a catastrophe for the boy. Matsumoto's place was only a sublet in any case, and Nathaniel and his friends will all find other apartments.

But it's such an ordeal in this city. And all four of the young people, however different they might be, strike Lucien as being in some kind of holding pattern—as if they're temporizing, or muffled by unspoken reservations. Of course, he doesn't really know them. Maybe it's just the eternal, poignant weariness of youth.

The strangest thing about getting old (or one of the many strangest things) is that young people sometimes appear to Lucien—as, in fact, Sharmila does at this very moment—in a nimbus of tender light. It's as if her unrealized future were projecting outward like ectoplasm.

"Doing anything entertaining this evening?" he asks her.

She sighs. "Time will tell," she says.

She's a nice young woman; he'd like to give her a few words of advice, or reassurance.

But what could they possibly be? "Don't—" he begins.

Don't worry? HAHAHAHAHA! Don't feel *sad*? "Don't bother about the phones," is what he settles down on. A new show goes up tomorrow, and it's become Lucien's custom on such evenings to linger in the stripped gallery and have a glass of wine. "I'll take care of them."

But how has he *gotten* so old?

SUSPENSION

So, there was the famous, strangely blank New Year's Eve, the nothing at all that happened, neither the apocalypse nor the failure of the planet's computers, nor, evidently, the dawning of a better age. Nathaniel had gone to parties with his old friends from school and was asleep before dawn; the next afternoon he awoke with only a mild hangover and an uneasy impression of something left undone.

Next thing you knew, along came that slump, as it was called—the general economic blight that withered the New York branch of Mr. Matsumoto's firm and clusters of jobs all over the city. There appeared to be no jobs at all, in fact, but then—somehow—Uncle Lucien unearthed one for Nathaniel in the architectural division of the subway system. It was virtually impossible to afford an apartment, but Uncle Lucien arranged for Nathaniel to sublet Mr. Matsumoto's loft.

Then Madison and his girlfriend broke up, so Madison moved into Mr. Matsumoto's, too. Not long afterward, the brokerage house where Amity was working collapsed resoundingly, and she'd joined them. Then Lyle's landlord jacked up his rent, so Lyle started living at Mr. Matsumoto's as well.

As the return of Mr. Matsumoto to New York was contingent upon the return of a reasonable business climate, one way or another it had sort of slipped their minds that Mr. Matsumoto was real. And for over three years there they've been, hanging in temporary splendor thirty-one floors above the pavement.

They're all out on the terrace this evening. Madison has brought in champagne so that they can salute with an adequate flourish the end of their tenure in Mr. Matsumoto's place. And except for Amity, who takes a principled stand against thoughtful moods, and Amity's new friend or possibly suitor, Russell, who has no history here, they're kind of quiet.

REUNION

Now that Sharmila has gone, Lucien's stunning, cutting-edge gallery space blurs a bit and recedes. The room, in fact, seems almost like an old snapshot from that bizarre, quaintly futuristic century, the twentieth. Lucien takes a bottle of white wine from the little fridge in the office, pours himself a glass, and from behind a door in that century, emerges Charlie.

Charlie—Oh, how long it's been, how unbearably long! Lucien luxuriates in the little pulse of warmth just under his skin that indicates her presence. He strains for traces of her voice, but her words degrade like the words in a dream, as if they're being rubbed through a sieve.

Yes, yes, Lucien assures her. He'll put his mind to finding another apartment for her nephew. And when her poor, exasperating sister and brother-in-law call frantically about Nathaniel, as they're bound to do, he'll do his best to calm them down.

But what a nuisance it all is! The boy is as opaque to his parents as a turnip. He was the child of their old age and he's also, obviously, the repository of all of their baroque hopes and fears. By their own account, they throw up their hands and wring them, lecture Nathaniel about frugality, then press spending money upon him and fret when he doesn't use it.

Between Charlie's death and Nathaniel's arrival in New York, Lucien heard from Rose and Isaac only at what they considered moments of emergency: Nathaniel's grades were erratic! His friends were bizarre! Nathaniel had expressed an interest in architecture, an unreliable future! He drew, and Lucien had better sit down, *comics*!

The lamentations would pour through the phone, and then, the instant Lucien hung up, evaporate. But if he had given the matter one moment's thought, he realizes, he would have understood from very early on that it was only a matter of time until the boy found his way to the city.

It was about four years ago now that Rose and Isaac put in an especially urgent call. Lucien held the receiver at arm's length and gritted his teeth. "You're an important man," Rose was shouting. "We understand that, we understand how busy you are, you know we'd never do this, but it's an emergency. The boy's in New York, and he sounds terrible. He doesn't have a job, lord only knows what he eats—I don't know what to think, Lucien, he *drifts*, he's just *drifting*. Call him, promise me, that's all I'm asking."

"Fine, certainly, good," Lucien said, already gabbling; he would have agreed to anything if Rose would only hang up.

"But whatever you do," she added, "please, please, under no circumstances should you let him know that we asked you to call."

Lucien looked at the receiver incredulously. "But how else would I have known he was in New York?" he said. "How else would I have gotten his number?"

There was a silence, and then a brief, amazed laugh from Isaac on another extension. "Well, I don't know what you'll tell him," Isaac said admiringly. "But you're the brains of the family, you'll think of something."

INNOCENCE

And actually, Russell (who seems to be not only Amity's friend and possible suitor but also her agent) has obtained for Amity a whopping big advance from some outfit that Madison refers to as Cheeseball Editions, so whatever else they might all be drinking to (or drinking about) naturally Amity's celebrating a bit. And Russell, recently arrived from L.A., cannot suppress his ecstasy about how *ur* New York, as he puts it, Mr. Matsumoto's loft is, tactless as he apparently recognizes this untimely ecstasy to be.

"It's *fantastic*," he says. "Who did it, do you know?"

Nathaniel nods. "Matthias Lehmann."

"That's what I thought, I thought so," Russell says. "It *looks* like Lehmann. Oh, wow, I can't believe you guys have to move out—I mean, it's just so totally amazing!"

Nathaniel and Madison nod and Lyle sniffs peevishly. Lyle is stretched out on a yoga mat that Nathaniel once bought in preparation for a romance (as yet manqué) with a prettily tattooed yoga teacher he runs into in the bodega on the corner. Lyle's skin has a waxy, bluish cast; there are dark patches beneath his eyes. He looks like a child too precociously worried to sleep. His boyfriend, Jahan, has more or less relocated to London, and Lyle has been missing him frantically. Lying there so still on the yoga mat with his eyes closed, he appears to be a tomb sculpture from an as yet nonexistent civilization.

"And the view!" Russell says. "This is probably the most incredible view on the *planet*."

The others consider the sight of Russell's eager face. And then Amity says, "More champagne, anyone?"

Well, sure, who knows where Russell had been? Who knows where he would have been on that shining, calm, perfectly blue September morning when the rest of them were here having coffee on the terrace and looked up at the annoying racket of a low-flying plane? Why should they expect Russell—now, nearly three years later—to imagine that moment out on the terrace when Lyle spilled his coffee and said, "Oh, shit," and something flashed and something tore, and the cloudless sky ignited.

HOME

Rose and Isaac have elbowed their way in behind Charlie, and no matter how forcefully Lucien tries to boot them out, they're making themselves at home, airing their dreary history.

Both sailed as tiny, traumatized children with their separate families and on separate voyages right into the Statue of Liberty's open arms. Rose was almost eleven when her little sister, Charlie, came into being, along with a stainless American birth certificate.

Neither Rose and Charlie's parents nor Isaac's ever recovered from their journey to the New World, to say nothing of what had preceded it. The two sets of old folks spoke, between them, Yiddish, Polish, Russian, German, Croatian, Slovenian, Ukrainian, Ruthenian, Rumanian, Latvian, Czech, and Hungarian, Charlie had once told Lucien, but not one of the four ever managed to learn more English than was needed to procure a quarter pound of smoked sturgeon from the deli. They worked impossible hours, they drank a little schnapps, and then, in due course, they died.

Isaac did fairly well manufacturing vacuum cleaners. He and Rose were solid members of their temple and the community, but, according to Charlie, no matter how uneventful their lives in the United States continued to be, filling out an unfamiliar form would cause Isaac's hands to sweat and send jets of acid through his innards. When he or Rose encountered someone in uniform—a train conductor, a meter maid, a crossing guard—their hearts would leap into their throats and they would think: *passport*!

Their three elder sons, Nathaniel's brothers, fulfilled Rose and Isaac's deepest hopes by turning out to be blindingly inconspicuous. The boys were so reliable and had so few characteristics it was hard to imagine what anyone could think up to kill them for. They were Jewish, of course, but even Rose and Isaac understood that this particular criterion was inoperative in the United States—at least for the time being.

The Old World, danger, and poverty were far in the past. Nevertheless, the family lived in their tidy, midwestern house with its two-car garage as if secret police were permanently hiding under the matching plastic-covered sofas, as if Brownshirts and Cossacks were permanently rampaging through the suburban streets.

Lucien knew precious little about vacuum cleaners and nothing at all about childhood infections or lawn fertilizers. And yet, as soon as Charlie introduced him, Isaac and Rose set about soliciting his views as if he were an authority on everything that existed on their shared continent.

His demurrals, disclaimers, and protestations of ignorance were completely ineffective. Whatever guess he was finally strong-armed into hazarding was received as oracular. Oracular!

Fervent gratitude was expressed: Thank God Charlie had brought Lucien into the family! How brilliant he was, how knowledgeable and subtle! And then Rose and Isaac would proceed to pick over his poor little opinion as if they were the most ruthless and highly trained lawyers, and on the opposing side.

After Charlie was diagnosed, Lucien had just enough time to understand perfectly what that was to mean. When he was exhausted enough to sleep, he slept as though under heavy anesthetic during an amputation. The pain was not alleviated, but it had been made inscrutable. A frightful thing seemed to lie on top of him, heavy and cold. All night long he would struggle to throw it off, but when dawn delivered him to consciousness, he understood what it was, and that it would never go away.

During his waking hours, the food on his plate would abruptly lose its taste, the painting he was studying would bleach off the canvas, the friend he was talking to would turn into a stranger. And then, one day, he was living in a world all made out of paper, where the sun was a wad of old newspapers and the only sounds were the sounds of tearing paper.

He spoke with Rose and Isaac frequently during Charlie's illness, and they came to New York for her memorial service, where they sat self-consciously and miserably among Lucien and Charlie's attractive friends. He took them to the airport for their return to the Midwest, embraced them warmly, and as they shuffled toward the departure door with the other passengers, turning once to wave, he breathed a sigh of relief: all that, at least, was over, too.

As his senses began to revive, he felt a brief pang—he would miss, in a minor way, the heartrending buffoonery of Charlie's sister and brother-in-law. After all, it had been part of his life with Charlie, even if it had been the only annoying part.

But Charlie's death, instead of setting him utterly, blessedly adrift in his grief, had left him anchored permanently offshore of her family like an island. After a long silence, the infuriating calls started up again. The feudal relationship was apparently inalterable.

CONTEXT

When they'd moved in, it probably *was* the best view on the planet. Then, one morning, out of a clear blue sky, it became, for a while, probably the worst.

For a long time now they've been able to hang out here on the terrace without anyone running inside to be sick or bursting into tears or diving under something at a loud noise or even just making macabre jokes or wondering what sort of debris is settling into their drinks. These days they rarely see—as for a time they invariably did—the sky igniting, the stinking smoke bursting out of it like lava, the tiny figures raining down from the shattered tower as Lyle faints.

But now it's unclear what they are, in fact, looking at.

INFORMATION

What would Charlie say about the show that's about to go up? It's work by a youngish Belgian painter who arrived, splashily, on the scene sometime after Charlie's departure.

It's good work, but these days Lucien can't get terribly excited about any of the shows. The vibrancy of his brain arranging itself in response to something of someone else's making, the heart's little leap—his gift, reliable for so many years, is gone. Or mostly gone; it's flattened out into something banal and tepid. It's as if he's got some part that's simply worn out and needs replacing. Let's hope it's still available, he thinks.

How *did* he get so old? The usual stupid question. One had snickered all one's life as the plaintive old geezers doddered about baffled, as if looking for a misplaced sock, tugging one's sleeve, asking sheepishly: *How did I get so old?*

The mere sight of one's patiently blank expression turned them vicious. *It will happen to you,* they'd raged.

Well, all right, it would. But not in the ridiculous way it had happened to *them*. And yet, here he is, he and his friends, falling like so much landfill into the dump of old age. Or at least struggling desperately to balance on the brink. Yet one second ago, running so swiftly toward it, they hadn't even seen it.

And what had happened to his youth? Unlike a misplaced sock, it isn't anywhere; it had dissolved in the making of him.

Surprising that after Charlie's death he did not take the irreversible step. He'd had no appetite to live. But the body has its own appetite, apparently—that pitiless need to continue with its living, which has so many disguises and so many rationales.

A deep embarrassment has been stalking him. Every time he lets his guard down these days, there it is. Because it's become clear: he and even the most dissolute among his friends have glided through their lives on the assumption that the sheer fact of their existence has in some way made the world a better place. As deranged as it sounds now, a better place. Not a leafy bower, maybe, but still, a somewhat better place— more tolerant, more amenable to the wonderful adventures of the human mind and the human body, more capable of outrage against injustice . . .

For shame! One has been shocked, all one's life, to learn of the blind eye turned to children covered with bruises and welts, the blind eye turned to the men who came at night for the neighbors. And yet . . . And yet one has clung to the belief that the sun shining inside one's head is evidence of sunshine elsewhere.

Not everywhere, of course. Obviously, at every moment something terrible is being done to someone somewhere—one can't really know about each instance of it!

Then again, how far away does something have to be before you have the right to not really know about it?

Sometime after Charlie's death, Lucien resumed throwing his parties. He and his friends continued to buy art and make art, to drink and reflect. They voted responsibly, they gave to charity, they read the paper assiduously. And while they were basking in their exclusive sunshine, what had happened to the planet? Lucien gazes at his glass of wine, his eyes stinging.

HOMESICK

Nathaniel was eight or nine when his aunt and uncle had come out to the Midwest to visit the family, lustrous and clever and comfortable and humorous and affectionate with one another, in their soft, stylish clothing. They'd brought books with them to read. When they talked to each other—and they habitually did—not only did they take turns, but also, what *one* said followed on what the *other* said. What world could they have come from? What was the world in which beings like his aunt and uncle could exist?

A world utterly unlike his parents', that was for sure—a world of freedom and lightness and beauty and the ardent exchange of ideas and . . . and . . . *fun.*

A great longing rose up in Nathaniel like a flower with a lovely, haunting fragrance. When he was ready, he'd thought—when he was able, when he was worthy, he'd get to the world from which his magic aunt and uncle had once briefly appeared.

The evidence, though, kept piling up that he was not worthy. Because even when he finished school, he simply didn't budge. How unfair it was—his friends had flown off so easily, as if going to New York were nothing at all.

Immediately after graduation, Madison found himself a job at a fancy New York PR firm. And it seemed that there was a place out there on the trading floor of the Stock Exchange for Amity. And Lyle had suddenly exhibited an astonishing talent for sound design and engineering, so where else would he sensibly live, either?

Yes, the fact was that only Nathaniel seemed slated to remain behind in their college town. Well, he told himself, his parents were getting on; he would worry, so far away. And he was actually employed as a part-time assistant with an actual architectural firm, whereas in New York the competition, for even the lowliest of such jobs, would be ferocious. And also, he had plenty of time, living where he did, to work on *Passivityman.*

And that's what he told Amity, too, when she'd called one night, four years ago, urging him to take the plunge.

"It's time for you to try, Nathaniel," she said. "It's time to commit. This oddball, slacker stance is getting kind of old, don't you think, kind of stale. You cannot let your life be ruled by fear any longer."

"Fear?" He flinched. "By what fear, exactly, do you happen to believe my life is ruled?"

"Well, I mean, fear of failure, obviously. Fear of mediocrity."

For an instant he thought he might be sick.

"Right," he said. "And why should I fear failure and mediocrity? Failure and mediocrity have such august traditions! Anyhow, what's up with you, Amity?"

She'd been easily distracted, and they chatted on for a while, but when they hung up, he felt very, very strange, as if his apartment had slightly changed shape. Amity was right, he'd thought; it was fear that stood between him and the life he'd meant to be leading.

That was probably the coldest night of the whole, difficult millennium. The timid midwestern sun had basically gone down at the beginning of September; it wouldn't be around much again till May. Black ice glared on the street outside like the cloak of an extra-cruel witch. The sink faucet was dripping into a cracked and stained teacup: *Tick tock tick tock . . .*

What was he *doing*? Once he'd dreamed of designing tranquil and ennobling dwellings, buildings that urged benign relationships, rich inner harmonies; he'd dreamed of meeting fascinating strangers. True, he'd managed to avoid certain pitfalls of middle-class adulthood—he wasn't a white-collar criminal, for example; he wasn't (at least as far as he knew) a total blowhard. But what was he *actually doing*? His most exciting social contact was the radio. He spent his salaried hours in a cinder-block office building, poring over catalogues of plumbing fixtures. The rest of the day—and the whole evening, too—he sat at the little desk his parents had bought for him when he was in junior high, slaving over *Passivityman,* a comic strip that ran in free papers all over parts of the Mid-west, a comic strip that was doted on by whole dozens, the fact was, of stoned undergrads.

He was twenty-four years old! Soon he'd be twenty-eight. In a few more minutes he'd be thirty-five, then fifty. Five zero. How had that happened? He was eighty! He could feel his vas-cular system and brain clogging with paste, he was drooling . . .

And if history had anything to teach, it was that he'd be broke when he was eighty, too, and that his personal life would still be a disaster.

But wait. Long ago, panic had sent his grandparents and parents scurrying from murderous Europe, with its death camps and pogroms, to the safe harbor of New York. Panic had kept them going as far as the Midwest, where grueling labor enabled them and eventually their children to lead blessedly ordinary lives. And sooner or later, Nathaniel's pounding heart was telling him, that same sure-footed guide, panic, would help him retrace his family's steps all the way back to Manhattan.

OPPORTUNISM

Blip! Charlie scatters again as Lucien's attention wavers from her and the empty space belonging to her is seized by Miss Mueller.

Huh, but what do you know—death *suits* Miss Mueller! In life she was drab, but now she absolutely throbs with ghoulishness. *You there, Lucien*—the shriek echoes around the gallery—*What are the world's three great religions?*

Zen Buddhism, Jainism, and Sufism, he responds sulkily.

Naughty boy! She cackles flirtatiously. *Bang bang, you're dead!*

THE HALF-LIFE OF PASSIVITY

Passivityman is taking a snooze, his standard response to stress, when the alarm rings. "I'll check it out later, boss," he murmurs.

"You'll check it out *now*, please," his girlfriend and superior, the beautiful Princess Prudence, tells him. "Just put on those grubby corduroys and get out there."

"Aw, is it really *urgent*?" he asks.

"Don't you get it?" she says. "I've been warning you, episode after episode! And now, from his appliance-rich house on the Moon, Captain Corporation has tightened his Net of Evil around the planet Earth, and he's dragging it out of orbit! The U.S. Congress is selected by pharmaceutical companies, the state of Israel is run by Christian fundamentalists, the folks that haul toxic sludge manufacture cattle feed and process burgers, your sources of news and information are edited by a giant mouse, New York City and Christian fundamentalism are holdings of a family in Kuwait—*and all of it's owned by Captain Corporation!*"

Passivityman rubs his eyes and yawns. "Well gosh, Pru, sure—but, like, what am I supposed to do about it?"

"*I* don't know," Princess Prudence says. "It's hardly my job to figure that out, is it? I mean, *you're* the superhero. Just—Just—just go out and do something conspicuously lacking in monetary value! Invent some stinky, profit-proof gloop to pour on stuff. Or, I don't know, whatever. But you'd better do *something*, before it's too late."

"Sounds like it's totally too late already," says Passivityman, reaching for a cigarette.

It was quite a while ago now that Passivityman seemed to throw in the towel. Nathaniel's friends looked at the strip with him and scratched their heads.

"Hm, I don't know, Nathaniel," Amity said. "This episode is awfully complicated. I mean, Passivityman's seeming kind of passive-*aggressive*, actually."

"Can Passivityman not be bothered any longer to protect the abject with his greed-repelling Shield of Sloth?" Lyle asked.

"It's not going to be revealed that Passivityman is a double agent, is it?" Madison said. "I mean, what about his undying struggle against corporate-model efficiency?"

"The truth is, I don't really know what's going on with him," Nathaniel said. "I was thinking that maybe, unbeknownst to himself, he's come under the thrall of his morally neutral, transgendering twin, Ambiguityperson."

"Yeah," Madison said. "But I mean, the problem here is that he's just not dealing with the paradox of his own being— he seems kind of *intellectually* passive . . ."

Oh, dear. Poor Passivityman. He was a *tired* old crime fighter. Nathaniel sighed; it was hard to live the way his superhero lived—constantly vigilant against the premature conclusion, scrupulously rejecting the vulgar ambition, rigorously deferring judgment and action . . . and all for the greater good.

"Huh, well, I guess he's sort of losing his superpowers," Nathaniel said.

The others looked away uncomfortably.

"Oh, it's probably just one of those slumps," Amity said. "I'm sure he'll be back to normal, soon."

But by now, Nathaniel realizes, he's all but stopped trying to work on *Passivityman*.

ALL THIS

Thanks for pointing that out, Miss Mueller. Yes, humanity seems to have reverted by a millennium or so. Goon squads, purporting to represent each of the *world's three great religions*— as they used to be called to fifth-graders, and perhaps still so misleadingly are—have deployed themselves all over the map, apparently in hopes of annihilating not only each other, but absolutely everyone, themselves excepted.

Just a few weeks earlier, Lucien was on a plane heading home from Los Angeles, and over the loudspeaker, the pilot requested that all Christians on board raise their hands. The next sickening instants provided more than enough time for conjecture as to who, exactly, was about to be killed— Christians or non-Christians. And then the pilot went on to ask those who had raised their hands to talk about their "faith" with the others.

Well, better him than Rose and Isaac; that would have been two sure heart attacks, right there. And anyhow, why should he be so snooty about religious fanaticism? Stalin managed to kill off over thirty million people in the name of no god at all, and not so very long ago.

———

At the moment when *all this*—as Lucien thinks of it—began, the moment when a few ordinary-looking men carrying box cutters sped past the limits of international negotiation and the frontiers of technology, turning his miraculous city into a nightmare and hurling the future into a void, Lucien was having his croissant and coffee.

The television was saying something. Lucien wheeled around and stared at it, then turned to look out the window; downtown, black smoke was already beginning to pollute the perfect, silken September morning. On the screen, the ruptured, flaming colossus was shedding veils of tiny black specks.

All circuits were busy, of course; the phone might as well have been a toy. Lucien was trembling as he shut the door of the apartment behind him. His face was wet. Outside, he saw that the sky in the north was still insanely blue.

THE AGE OF DROSS

Well, superpowers are probably a feature of youth, like Wendy's ability to fly around with that creepy Peter Pan. Or maybe they belonged to a loftier period of history. It seems that Captain Corporation, his swaggering lieutenants and massed armies have actually neutralized Passivityman's superpower. Passivityman's astonishing reserves of resistance have vanished in the quicksand of Captain Corporation's invisible account books. His rallying cry, No way, which once rang out over the land, demobilizing millions, has been altered by Captain Corporation's co-optophone into, Whatever. And the superpowers of Nathaniel's friends have been seriously challenged, too. Challenged, or . . . outgrown.

Amity's superpower, her gift for exploiting systemic weaknesses, had taken a terrible beating several years ago when the gold she spun out on the trading floor turned—just like everyone else's—into straw. And subsequently, she plummeted from job to job, through layers of prestige, ending up behind a counter in a fancy department store where she sold overpriced skin-care products.

Now, of course, the sale of *Inner Beauty Secrets*—her humorous, lightly fictionalized account of her experiences there with her clients—indicates that perhaps her powers are regenerating. But time will tell.

Madison's superpower, an obtuse, patrician equanimity in the face of damning fact, was violently and irremediably terminated one day when a girl arrived at the door asking for him.

"I'm your sister," she told him. "Sorry," Madison said, "I've never seen you before in my life." "Hang on," the girl said. "I'm just getting to that."

For months afterward, Madison kept everyone awake late into the night repudiating all his former beliefs, his beautiful blue eyes whirling around and his hair standing on end as if he'd stuck his hand into a socket. He quit his lucrative PR job and denounced the firm's practices in open letters to media watchdog groups (copies to his former boss). The many women who'd been running after him did a fast about-face.

Amity called him a "bitter skeptic"; he called Amity a "dupe." The heated quarrel that followed has tapered off into an uneasy truce, at best.

Lyle's superpower back in school was his spectacular level of aggrievedness and his ability to get anyone at all to feel sorry for him. But later, doing sound with a Paris-based dance group, Lyle met Jahan, who was doing the troupe's lighting.

Jahan is (a) as handsome as a prince, (b) as charming, as

intelligent, as noble in his thoughts, feelings, and actions as a prince, and (c) a prince, at least of some attenuated sort. So no one feels sorry for Lyle at all any longer, and Lyle has apparently left the pleasures of even *self*-pity behind him without a second thought.

Awhile ago, though, Jahan was mistakenly arrested in some sort of sweep near Times Square, and when he was finally released from custody, he moved to London, and Lyle does nothing but pine, when he can't be in London himself.

"Well, look on the bright side," Nathaniel said. "At least you might get your superpower back."

"You know, Nathaniel . . ." Lyle said. He looked at Nathaniel for a moment, and then an unfamiliar kindness modified his expression. He patted Nathaniel on the shoulder and went on his way.

Yikes. So much for Lyle's superpower, obviously.

"It's great that you got to live here for so long, though," Russell is saying.

Nathaniel has the sudden sensation of his whole four years in New York twisting themselves into an arrow, speeding through the air and twanging into the dead center of this evening. All so hard to believe. "This is not happening," he says.

"I think it might really *be* happening, though," Lyle says.

"Fifty percent of respondents say that the event taking place is not occurring," Madison says. "The other fifty percent remain undecided. Clearly, the truth lies somewhere in between."

Soon it might be as if he and Lyle and Madison and Amity had never even lived here. Because this moment is joined to all the other moments they've spent together here, and all of those moments are Right Now. But soon this moment and all the others will be cut off—in the past, not part of Right Now at all. Yeah, he and his three friends might all be going their separate ways, come to think of it, once they move out.

CONTINUITY

While the sirens screamed, Lucien had walked against the tide of dazed, smoke-smeared people, down into the fuming cauldron, and when he finally reached the police cordon, his feet aching, he wandered along it for hours, searching for Charlie's nephew, among all the other people who were searching for family, friends, lovers.

Oh, that day! One kept waiting—as if a morning would arrive from before that day to take them all along a different track. One kept waiting for that shattering day to unhappen, so that the real—the intended—future, the one that had been implied by the past, could unfold. Hour after hour, month after month, waiting for that day to not have happened. But it had happened. And now it was always going to have happened.

Most likely on the very mornings that first Rose and then Isaac had disembarked at Ellis Island, each clutching some remnant of the world they were never to see again, Lucien was being wheeled in his pram through the genteel world, a few miles uptown, of brownstones.

The city, more than his body, contained his life. His

life! The schools he had gone to as a child, the market where his mother had bought the groceries, the park where he had played with his classmates, the restaurants where he had courted Charlie, the various apartments they'd lived in, the apartments of their friends, the gallery, the newsstand on the corner, the dry cleaner's . . . The things he did in the course of the day, year after year, the people he encountered.

A sticky layer of crematorium ash settled over the whole of Matsumoto's neighborhood, even inside, behind closed windows, as thick in places as turf, and water was unavailable for a time. Nathaniel and his friends all stayed elsewhere, of course, for a few weeks. When it became possible, Lucien sent crews down to Matsumoto's loft to scour the place and restore the art.

FAREWELL

A memorandum hangs in Mr. Matsumoto's lobby, that appeared several months ago when freakish blackouts were rolling over the city.

Emergency Tips from the Management urges residents to assemble a Go Bag, in the event of an evacuation, as well as an In-Home Survival Kit. Among items to include: a large amount of cash in small denominations, water and nonperishable foods such as granola bars, a wind-up radio, warm clothing and sturdy walking shoes, unscented bleach and an eyedropper for purifying water, plastic sheeting and duct tape, a whistle, a box cutter.

Also recommended is a Household Disaster Plan and the practicing of emergency drills.

A hand-lettered sign next to the elevator says THINK TWICE.

Twenty-eight years old, no superhero, a job that just *might* lead down to a career in underground architecture, a vanishing apartment, a menacing elevator . . . Maybe he should view Mr. Matsumoto's return as an opportunity, and regroup. Maybe he should *do* something—take matters in hand. Maybe he should go try to find Delphine, for example.

But how? He hasn't heard from her, and she could be anywhere now; she'd mentioned Bucharest, she'd mentioned Havana, she'd mentioned Shanghai, she'd mentioned Istanbul . . .

He'd met her at one his uncle's parties. There was the usual huge roomful of people wearing strangely pleated black clothes, like the garments of a somber devotional sect, and there she was in electric-blue taffeta, amazingly tall and narrow, lazy and nervous, like an electric bluebell.

She favored men nearly twice Nathaniel's age and millions of times richer, but for a while she let Nathaniel come over to her apartment and play her his favorite CDs. They drank perfumey infusions from chipped porcelain cups, or vodka. Delphine could become thrillingly drunk, and she smoked, letting long columns of ash form on her tarry, unfiltered cigarettes. One night, when he lost his keys, she let him come over and sleep in her bed while she went out, and when the sky fell, she actually let him sleep on her floor for a week.

Her apartment was filled with puffy, silky little sofas, and old, damaged mirrors and tarnished candlesticks, and tall vases filled with slightly wilting flowers. It smelled like powder and tea and cigarettes and her Abyssinian cats, which prowled the savannas of the white, long-haired rugs or posed on the marble mantelpiece.

Delphine's father was Armenian and he lived in Paris, which according to Delphine was a bore. Her mother was Chilean. Delphine's English had been acquired at a boarding school in Kent for dull-witted rich girls and castaways, like herself, from everywhere.

She spoke many languages, she was self-possessed and beautiful and fascinating. She could have gone to live anywhere. And she had come, like Nathaniel, to New York.

"But look at it now," she'd raged. Washington was dropping bombs on Afghanistan and then Iraq, and every few weeks there was a flurry of alerts in kindergarten colors indicating the likelihood of terrorist attacks: yellow, orange, red, *duck*!

"Do you know how I get the news here?" Delphine said. "From your newspapers? Please! From your newspapers I learn what restaurant has opened. News I learn in taxis, from the drivers. And how do they get it? From their friends and relatives back home, in Pakistan or Uzbekistan or Somalia. The drivers sit around at the airport, swapping information, and they can tell you *anything*. But do you ask? Or sometimes I talk to my friends in Europe. Do you know what they're saying about you over there?"

"Please don't say 'you,' Delphine," he had said faintly.

"Oh, yes, here it's not like stuffy old Europe, where everything is stifled by tradition and trauma. Here you're able to speak freely, within reason, of course, and isn't it wonderful that you all happen to want to say exactly what they want you to say? Do you know how many people you're killing over there? No, how would you? Good, just keep your eyes closed, panic, don't ask any questions, and you can speak freely about whatever you like. And if you have any suspicious-looking neighbors, be sure to tell the police. You had everything here, everything, and you threw it all away in one second."

She was so beautiful; he'd gazed at her as if he were already remembering her. "Please don't say 'you,'" he murmured again.

"Poor Nathaniel," she said. "This place is nothing now but a small-minded, mean-spirited provincial town."

THE AGE OF DIGITAL REASONING

One/two. On/off. The plane crashes/doesn't crash.

The plane he took from L.A. didn't crash. It wasn't used as a missile to blow anything up, and not even one passenger was shot or stabbed. Nothing happened. So, what's the problem? What's the difference between having been on that flight and having been on any other flight in his life?

Oh, what's the point of thinking about death all the time! Think about it or not, you die. Besides—and here's something that sure hasn't changed—you don't have to do it more than once. And as you don't have to do it *less* than once, either, you might as well do it on the plane. Maybe there's no special problem these days. Maybe the problem is just that he's old.

Or maybe his nephew's is the last generation that will remember what it had once felt like to blithely assume there would be a future—at least a future like the one that had been implied by the past they'd all been familiar with.

But the future actually ahead of them, it's now obvious, had itself been implied by a past; and the terrible day that pointed them toward that future had been prepared for a long, long time, though it had been prepared behind a curtain.

It was as if there had been a curtain, a curtain painted with the map of the earth, its oceans and continents, with Lucien's delightful city. The planes struck, tearing through the curtain of that blue September morning, exposing the dark world that lay right behind it, of populations ruthlessly exploited, inflamed with hatred, and tired of waiting for change to happen by.

The stump of the ruined tower continued to smolder far into the fall, and an unseasonable heat persisted. When the smoke lifted, all kinds of other events, which had been prepared behind a curtain, too, were revealed. Flags waved in the brisk air of fear, files were demanded from libraries and hospitals, droning helicopters hung over the city, and heavily armed policemen patrolled the parks. Meanwhile, one read that executives had pocketed the savings of their investors and the pensions of their employees.

The wars in the East were hidden behind a thicket of language: *patriotism, democracy, loyalty, freedom*—the words bounced around, changing purpose, as if they were made out of some funny plastic. What did they actually refer to? It seemed that they all might refer to money.

Were the sudden power outages and spiking level of unemployment related? And what was causing them? The newspapers seemed for the most part to agree that the cause of both was terrorism. But lots of people said they were both the consequence of corporate theft. It was certainly all beyond Lucien! Things that had formerly appeared to be distinct, or even at odds, now seemed to have been smoothly blended, to mutual advantage. Provocation and retribution, arms manufacture and statehood, oil and war, commerce and dogma, and the spinning planet seemed to be boiling them all together at the center of the earth into a poison syrup. Enemies had soared toward each other from out of the past to unite in a joyous fireball; planes had sheared through the heavy, painted curtain and from the severed towers an inexhaustible geyser had erupted.

Styles of pets revolved rapidly, as if the city's residents were searching for a type of animal that would express a stance appropriate to the horrifying assault, which for all anyone knew was only the first of many.

For a couple of months everyone was walking cute, perky things. Then Lucien saw snarling hounds everywhere and the occasional boa constrictor draped around its owner's shoulders. After that, it was tiny, trembling dogs that traveled in purses and pockets.

New York had once been the threshold of an impregnable haven, then the city had become in an instant the country's open wound, and now it was the occasion—the pretext!—for killing and theft and legislative horrors all over the world. The air stank from particulate matter—chemicals and asbestos and blood and scorched bone. People developed coughs and strange rashes.

What should be done, and to whom? Almost any word, even between friends, could ignite a sheet of flame. What were the bombings for? First one imperative was cited and then another; the rationales shifted hastily to cover successive gaps in credibility. Bills were passed containing buried provisions, and loopholes were triumphantly discovered—alarming elasticities or rigidities in this law or that. One was sick of trying to get a solid handle on the stream of pronouncements—it was like endlessly trying to sort little bits of paper into stacks when a powerful fan was on.

Friends in Europe and Asia sent him clippings about his own country. *What's all this,* they asked—secret arrests and detentions, his president capering about in military uniform, crazy talk of preemptive nuclear strikes? Why were they releasing a big science fiction horror movie over there, about the emperor of everything everywhere, for which the whole world was required to buy tickets? What on earth was going on with them all, why were they all so silent? Why did they all seem so confused?

How was he to know, Lucien thought. If his foreign friends had such great newspapers, why didn't *they* tell *him*!

No more smiles from strangers on the street! Well, it was reasonable to be frightened; everyone had seen what those few men were able do with the odds and ends in their pockets. The heat lifted, and then there was unremitting cold. No one lingered to joke and converse in the course of their errands, but instead hurried irritably along, like people with bad consciences.

And always in front of you now was the sight that had been hidden by the curtain, of all those irrepressibly, murderously angry people.

———

Private life shrank to nothing. All one's feelings had been absorbed by an arid wasteland—policy, strategy, goals. One's past, one's future, one's ordinary daily pleasures were like dusty little curios on a shelf.

Lucien continued defiantly throwing his parties, but as the murky wars dragged on, he stopped. It was impossible to have fun or to want to have fun. It was one thing to have fun if the sun was shining generally, quite another thing to have fun if it was raining blood everywhere but on your party. What did he and his friends really have in common, anyway? Maybe nothing more than their level of privilege.

In restaurants and cafes all over the city, people seemed to have changed. The good-hearted, casually wasteful festival was over. In some places the diners were sullen and dogged, as if they felt accused of getting away with something.

In other places, the gaiety was cranked up to the level of completely unconvincing hysteria. For a long miserable while, in fact, the city looked like a school play about war profiteering. The bars were overflowing with very young people from heaven only knew where, in hideous, ludicrously showy clothing, spending massive amounts of money on green, pink, and orange cocktails, and laughing at the top of their lungs, as if at filthy jokes.

No, not like a school play—like a movie, though the performances and the direction were crude. The loud, ostensibly carefree young people appeared to be extras recruited from the suburbs, and yet sometime in the distant future, people seeing such a movie might think oh, yes, that was a New York that existed once, say, at the end of the millennium.

It was Lucien's city, Lucien's times, and yet what he appeared to be living in wasn't the actual present—it was an inaccurate representation of the *past*. True, it looked something like the New York that existed before *all this* began, but Lucien remembered, and he could see: the costumes were not quite right, the hairstyles were not quite right, the gestures and the dialogue were not quite right.

Oh. Yes. Of course none of it was quite right—the movie was a *propaganda* movie. And now it seems that the propaganda movie has done its job; things, in a grotesque sense, are back to normal.

Money is flowing a bit again, most of the flags have folded up, those nerve-wracking terror alerts have all but stopped, the kids in the restaurants have calmed down, no more rolling blackouts, and the dogs on the street encode no particular messages. Once again, people are concerned with getting on with their lives. Once again, the curtain has dropped.

Except that people seem a little bit nervous, a little uncomfortable, a little wary. Because you can't help sort of knowing that what you're seeing is only the curtain. And you can't help guessing what might be going on behind it.

THE FURTHER IN THE PAST THINGS ARE, THE BIGGER THEY BECOME

Nathaniel remembers more and more rather than less and less vividly the visit of his uncle and aunt to the Midwest during his childhood.

He'd thought his aunt Charlie was the most beautiful woman he'd ever seen. And for all he knows, she really was. He never saw her after that one visit; by the time he came to New York and reconnected with Uncle Lucien she had been dead for a long time. She would still have been under fifty when she died—crushed, his mother had once, in a mood, implied, by the weight of her own pretensions.

His poor mother! She had cooked, cleaned, and fretted for . . . months, it had seemed, in preparation for that visit of Uncle Lucien and Aunt Charlie. And observing in his memory the four grown-ups, Nathaniel can see an awful lot of white knuckles.

He remembers his mother picking up a book Aunt Charlie had left lying on the kitchen table, glancing at it and putting it back down with a tiny shrug and a lifted eyebrow. "You don't approve?" Aunt Charlie said, and Nathaniel is shocked to see, in his memory, that she is tense.

His mother, having gained the advantage, makes another bitter little shrug. "I'm sure it's over my head," she says.

When the term of the visit came to an end, they dropped Uncle Lucien and Aunt Charlie at the airport. His brother was driving, too fast. Nathaniel can hear himself announcing in his child's piercing voice, "*I want to live in New York like Uncle Lucien and Aunt Charlie!*" His exile's heart was brimming, but it was clear from his mother's profile that she was braced for an execution.

"Slow *down*, Bernie!" his mother said, but Bernie hadn't. "Big shot," she muttered, though it was unclear at whom this was directed—whether at his brother or himself or his father, or his Uncle Lucien, or at Aunt Charlie herself.

BACK TO NORMAL

Do dogs have to fight sadness as tirelessly as humans do? They seem less involved with retrospect, less involved in dread and anticipation. Animals other than humans appear to be having a more profound experience of the present. But who's to say? Clearly their feelings are intense, and maybe grief and anxiety darken all their days. Maybe that's why they've acquired their stripes and polka dots and fluffiness—to cheer themselves up.

Poor old Earth, an old sponge, a honeycomb of empty mine shafts and dried wells. While he and his friends were wittering on, the planet underfoot had been looted. The waterways glint with weapons-grade plutonium, sneaked on barges between one wrathful nation and another, the polar ice caps melt, Venice sinks.

In the horrible old days in Europe when Rose and Isaac were hunted children, it must have been pretty clear to them how to behave, minute by minute. Men in jackboots? Up to the attic!

But even during that time when it was so dangerous to speak out, to act courageously, heroes emerged. Most of them died fruitlessly, of course, and unheralded. But now there are even monuments to some of them, and information about such people is always coming to light.

Maybe there really is no problem, maybe everything really is back to normal and maybe the whole period will sink peacefully away, to be remembered only by scholars. But if it should end, instead, in dire catastrophe, whom will the monuments of the future commemorate?

Today, all day long, Lucien has seen the president's vacant, stricken expression staring from the ubiquitous television screens. He seemed to be talking about positioning weapons in space, colonizing the moon.

Open your books to page 167, class, Miss Mueller shrieks. *What do you see?*

Lucien sighs.

The pages are thin and sort of shiny. The illustrations are mostly black and white.

This one's a photograph of a statue, an emperor, apparently, wearing his stone toga and his stone wreath. The real people, the living people, mill about just beyond the picture's confines, but Lucien knows more or less what they look like—he's seen illustrations of them, too. He knows what a viaduct is and that the ancient Romans went to plays and banquets and that they had a code of law from which his country's own is derived. Are the people hidden by the picture frightened? Do they hear the stones working themselves loose, the temples and houses and courts beginning to crumble?

Out the window, the sun is just a tiny, tiny bit higher today than it was at this exact instant yesterday. After school, he and Robbie Stern will go play soccer in the park. In another month it will be bright and warm.

PARADISE

So, Mr. Matsumoto will be coming back, and things seem pretty much as they did when he left. The apartment is clean, the cats are healthy, the art is undamaged, and the view from the terrace is exactly the same, except there's that weird, blank spot where the towers used to stand.

"Open the next?" Madison says, holding up a bottle of champagne. "Strongly agree, agree, undecided, disagree, strongly disagree."

"Strongly agree," Lyle says.

"Thanks," Amity says.

"Okay," Russell says. "I'm in."

Nathaniel shrugs and holds out his glass.

Madison pours. "Polls indicate that 100 percent of the American public approves heavy drinking," he says.

"Oh, god, Madison," Amity says. "Can't we ever just *drop* it? Can't we ever just have a nice time?"

Madison looks at her for a long moment. "Drop what?" he says, evenly.

But no one wants to get into *that*.

When Nathaniel was in his last year at college, his father began to suffer from heart trouble. It was easy enough for Nathaniel to come home on the weekends, and he'd sit with his father, gazing out the window as the autumnal light gilded the dry grass and the fallen leaves glowed.

His father talked about his own time at school, working night and day, the pride his parents had taken in him, the first college student in their family.

Over the years Nathaniel's mother and father had grown gentler with one another and with him. Sometimes after dinner and the dishes, they'd all go out for a treat. Nathaniel would wait, an acid pity weakening his bones, while his parents debated worriedly over their choices, as if nobody ever had before or would ever have again the opportunity to eat ice cream.

Just last night, he dreamed about Delphine, a delicious champagne-style dream, full of love and beauty—a weird, high-quality love, a feeling he doesn't remember ever having had in his waking life—a pure, wholehearted, shining love.

It hangs around him still, floating through the air out on the terrace—fragrant, shimmering, fading.

WAITING

The bell is about to ring. Closing his book Lucien hears the thrilling crash as the bloated empire tumbles down.

Gold star, Lucien! Miss Mueller cackles deafeningly, and then she's gone.

Charlie's leaving, too. Lucien lifts his glass; she glances back across the thin, inflexible divide.

From farther than the moon she sees the children of some distant planet study pictures in their text: there's Rose and Isaac at their kitchen table, Nathaniel out on Mr. Matsumoto's terrace, Lucien alone in the dim gallery—and then the children turn the page.

SOME OTHER, BETTER OTTO

"I don't know why I committed us to any of those things," Otto said. "I'd much prefer to be working or reading, and you'll want all the time you can get this week to practice."

"It's fine with me," William said. "I always like to see Sharon. And we'll survive the evening with your—"

Otto winced.

"Well, we will," William said. "And don't you want to see Naomi and Margaret and the baby as soon as they get back?"

"Everyone always says, 'Don't you want to see the baby, don't you want to see the baby,' but if I did want to see a fat, bald, confused person, obviously I'd have only to look in the mirror."

"I was reading a remarkable article in the paper this morning about holiday depression," William said. "Should I clip it for you? The statistics were amazing."

"The statistics cannot have been amazing, the article cannot have been remarkable, and I am not 'depressed.' I just happen to be bored sick by these inane— Waving our little antennae, joining our little paws in indication of— Oh, what is the point? Why did I agree to any of this?"

"Well," William said. "I mean, this is what we do."

———

Hmm. Well, true. And the further truth was, Otto saw, that he himself wanted, in some way, to see Sharon; he himself wanted, in some way, to see Naomi and Margaret and the baby as soon as possible. And it was even he himself who had agreed to join his family for Thanksgiving. It would be straining some concept—possibly the concept of "wanted," possibly the concept of "self"—to say that he himself had wanted to join them, and yet there clearly must have been an implicit alternative to joining them that was even less desirable, or he would not, after all, have agreed to it.

It had taken him—how long?—years and years to establish a viable, if not pristine, degree of estrangement from his family. Which was no doubt why, he once explained to William, he had tended, over the decades, to be so irascible and easily exhausted. The sustained effort, the subliminal concentration that was required to detach the stubborn prehensile hold was enough to wear a person right out and keep him from ever getting down to anything of real substance.

Weddings had lapsed entirely, birthdays were a phone call at the most, and at Christmas, Otto and William sent lavish gifts of out-of-season fruits, in the wake of which would arrive recriminatory little thank-you notes. From mid-December to mid-January they would absent themselves, not merely from the perilous vicinity of Otto's family, but from the entire country, to frolic in blue water under sunny skies.

When his mother died, Otto experienced an exhilarating melancholy; most of the painful encounters and obligations would now be a thing of the past. Life, with its humorous theatricality, had bestowed and revoked with one gesture, and there he abruptly was, in the position he felt he'd been born for: he was alone in the world.

Or alone in the world, anyway, with William. Marching ahead of his sisters and brother—Corinne, Martin, and Sharon—Otto was in the front ranks now, death's cannon fodder and so on; he had become old overnight, and free.

Old and free! Old and free . . .

Still, he made himself available to provide legal advice or to arrange a summer internship for some child or nephew. He saw Sharon from time to time. From time to time there were calls: "Of course you're too busy, but . . ." "Of course you're not interested, but . . ." was how they began. This was the one thing Corinne and her husband and Martin and whichever wife were always all in accord about—that Otto seemed to feel he was too good for the rest of them, despite the obvious indications to the contrary.

Who was too good for whom? It often came down to a show of force. When Corinne had called a week or so earlier about Thanksgiving, Otto, addled by alarm, said, "We're having people ourselves, I'm afraid."

Corinne's silence was like a mirror, flashing his tiny, harmless lie back to him in huge magnification, all covered with sticky hairs and microbes.

"Well, I'll see what I can do," he said.

"Please try," Corinne said. The phrase had the unassailable authority of a road sign appearing suddenly around the bend: FALLING ROCK. "Otto, the children are growing up."

"Children! What children? Your children grew up years ago, Corinne. Your children are old now, like us."

"I meant, of course, Martin's. The new ones. Martin and Laurie's. And there's Portia."

Portia? Oh, yes. The little girl. The sole, thank heavens, issue, of Martin's marriage to that crazy Viola.

"I'll see what I can do," Otto said again, this time less

cravenly. It was Corinne's own fault. A person of finer sensibil-
ities would have written a note, or used e-mail—or would
face-savingly have left a message at his office, giving him time
to prepare some well-crafted deterrent rather than whatever
makeshift explosive he would obviously be forced to lob back
at her under direct attack.

"Wesley and I are having it in the city this year," Corinne
was saying. "No need to come all the way out to the nasty
country. A few hours and it will all be over with. Seriously,
Otto, you're an integral element. We're keeping it simple this
year."

" 'This year?' Corinne, there have been no other years.
You do not observe Thanksgiving."

"In fact, Otto, we do. And we all used to."

"Who?"

"All of us."

"Never. When? Can you imagine Mother being thankful
for anything?"

"We always celebrated Thanksgiving when Father was
alive."

"I remember no such thing."

"I do. I remember, and so does Martin."

"Martin was four when Father died!"

"Well, you were little, too."

"I was twice Martin's age."

"Oh, Otto—I just feel sad, sometimes, to tell you the
truth, don't you? It's all going so fast! I'd like to see everyone
in the same room once a century or so. I want to see everybody well and happy. I mean, you and Martin and Sharon
were my brothers and sister. What was *that* all about? Don't
you remember? Playing together all the time?"

"I just remember Martin throwing up all the time."

"You'll be nice to him, won't you, Otto? He's still very sensitive. He won't want to talk about the lawsuit."

"Have you spoken to Sharon?"

"Well, that's something I wanted to talk to you about, actually. I'm afraid I might have offended her. I stressed the fact that it was only to be us this year. No aunts or uncles, no cousins, no friends. Just us. And husbands or wives. Husband. And wife. Or whatever. And children, naturally, but she became very hostile."

"Assuming William to be 'whatever,' " Otto said, "why shouldn't Sharon bring a friend if she wants to?"

"William is *family*. And surely you remember when she brought that person to Christmas! The person with the feet? I wish you'd go by and talk to her in the next few days. She seems to listen to you."

Otto fished up a magazine from the floor—one of the popular science magazines William always left lying around—and idly opened it.

"Wesley and I reach out to her," Corinne was saying. "And so does Martin, but she doesn't respond. I know it can be hard for her to be with people, but we're not people—we're family."

"I'm sure she understands that, Corinne."

"I hope you do, too, Otto."

How clearly he could see, through the phone line, this little sister of his—in her fifties now—the six-year-old's expression of aggrieved anxiety long etched decisively on her face.

"In any case," she said, "I've called."

And yet there was something to what Corinne had said; they had been one another's environs as children. The distance between them had been as great, in any important way, as it was now, but there had been no other beings close by, no other beings through whom they could probe or illumine the mystifying chasms and absences and yearnings within themselves. They had been born into the arid clutter of one another's behavior, good and bad, their measles, skinned knees, report cards . . .

A barren landscape dotted with clutter. Perhaps the life of the last dinosaurs, as they ranged, puzzled and sorrowful, across the comet-singed planet, was similar to childhood. It hadn't been a pleasant time, surely, and yet one did have an impulse to acknowledge one's antecedents, now and again. Hello, that was us, it still is, good-bye.

"I don't know," William said. "It doesn't seem fair to put any pressure on Sharon."

"Heaven forfend. But I did promise Corinne I'd speak with Sharon. And, after all, I haven't actually seen her for some time."

"We could just go have a plain old visit, though. I don't know. Urging her to go to Corinne's—I'm not really comfortable with that."

"Oof, William, phrase, please, jargon."

"Why is that jargon?"

"Why? How should I know why? Because it is. You can say, 'I'm uncomfortable *about* that,' or 'That makes me uncomfortable.' But 'I'm uncomfortable *with* that' is simply jargon." He picked up a book sitting next to him on the table and opened it. *Relativity for Dummies*. "Good heavens," he said, snapping the book shut. "*Obviously* Martin doesn't want to talk about the lawsuit. Why bother to mention that to me? Does she think I'm going to ask Martin whether it's true that he's been misrepresenting the value of his client's stock? Am

I likely to talk about it? I'm perfectly happy to read about it in the *Times* every day, like everyone else."

"You know," William said, "we could go away early this year. We could just pick up and leave on Wednesday, if you'd like."

"I would not like. I would like you to play in your concert, as always."

William took the book from Otto and held Otto's hand between his own. "They're not really so bad, you know, your family," he said.

Sometimes William's consolations were oddly like provocations. "Easy for you to say," Otto said.

"Not that easy."

"I'm sorry," Otto said. "I know."

Just like William to suggest going away early for Otto's sake, when he looked forward so much to his concert! The little orchestra played publicly only once a year, the Sunday after Thanksgiving. Otto endured the grating preparatory practicing, not exactly with equanimity, it had to be admitted, but with relative forbearance, just for the pleasure of seeing William's radiant face on the occasion. William in his suit, William fussing over the programs, William busily arranging tickets for friends. Otto's sunny, his patient, his deeply good William. Toward the end of every year, when the city lights glimmered through the fuzzy winter dark, on the Sunday after Thanksgiving, William with his glowing violin, urging the good-natured, timid audience into passionate explorations of the unseen world. And every year now, from the audience, Otto felt William's impress stamped on the planet, more legible and valuable by one year; all the more legible and valuable for the one year's diminution in William's beauty.

How spectacular he had been the first time Otto brought him to a family event, that gladiatorial Christmas thirty-odd years earlier. How had Otto ever marshaled the nerve to do it?

Oh, one could say till one was blue in the face that Christmas was a day like any other, what difference would it make if he and William were to spend that particular day apart, and so on. And yet.

Yes, the occasion forced the issue, didn't it. Either he and William would both attend, or Otto would attend alone, or they would not attend together. But whatever it was that one decided to do, it would be a declaration—to the family, and to the other. And, the fact was, to oneself.

Steeled by new love, in giddy defiance, Otto had arrived at the house with William, to all intents and purposes, on his arm.

A tidal wave of nervous prurience had practically blown the door out from inside the instant he and William ascended the front step. And all evening aunts, uncles, cousins, mother, and siblings had stared at William beadily, as if a little bunny had loped out into a clearing in front of them.

William's beauty, and the fact that he was scarcely twenty, had embarrassed Otto on other occasions, but never so searingly. "How *intelligent* he is!" Otto's relatives kept whispering to one another loudly, meaning, apparently, that it was a marvel he could speak. Unlike, the further implication was, the men they'd evidently been imagining all these years.

Otto had brought someone to a family event only once before—also on a Christmas, with everyone in attendance: Diandra Fetlin, a feverishly brilliant colleague, far less beautiful than William. During the turkey, she thumped Otto on the arm whenever he made a good point in the argument he was having with Wesley, and continued to eat with solemn assiduity. Then, while the others applied themselves to dessert, a stuccolike fantasy requiring vigilance, Diandra had delivered an explication of one of the firm's recent cases that was worth three semesters of law school. No one commented on *her* intelligence. And no one had been in the least deceived by Otto's tepid display of interest in her.

"So," Corinne had said in a loud and artificially genial tone as if she were speaking to an armed high-school student, "where did you and William meet, Otto?"

The table fell silent; Otto looked out at the wolfish ring of faces. "On Third Avenue," he said distinctly, and returned to his meal.

"Sorry," he said, as he and William climbed into the car afterward. "Sorry to have embarrassed you. Sorry to have shocked them. Sorry, sorry, sorry. But what was I supposed to say? All that completely fraudulent *interest*. The *solicitude*. The truth is, they've *never* sanctioned my way of life. Or, alternately, they've always *sanctioned* it. Oh, what on earth good is it to have a word that means only itself and its opposite!"

Driving back to the city, through the assaultively scenic and demographically uniform little towns, they were silent. William had witnessed; his power over Otto had been substantially increased by the preceding several hours, and yet he was exhibiting no signs of triumph. On the contrary, his habitual chipper mood was—where? Simply eclipsed. Otto glanced at him; no glance was returned.

Back in the apartment, they sat for a while in the dark.

Tears stung Otto's eyes and nose. He would miss William terribly. "It was a mistake," he said.

William gestured absently. "Well, we had to do it sooner or later."

We? We did? It was as if snow had begun to fall in the apartment—a gentle, chiming, twinkling snow. And sitting there, looking at one another silently, it became apparent that what each was facing was his future.

Marvelous to watch William out in the garden, now with the late chrysanthemums. It was a flower Otto had never liked until William instructed him to look again. Well, all right, so it wasn't a merry flower. But flowers could comfortably embrace a range of qualities, it seemed. And now, how Otto loved the imperial colors, the tensely arched blossoms, the cleansing scent that seemed dipped up from the pure well of winter, nature's ceremony of end and beginning.

The flat little disk of autumn sun was retreating, high up over the neighbors' buildings. As Otto gazed out the window, William straightened, shaded his eyes, waved, and bent back to work. Late in the year, William in the garden . . .

Otto bought the brownstone when he and William had decided to truly move in together. Over twenty-five years ago, that was. The place was in disrepair and cost comparatively little at the time. While Otto hacked his way through the barbed thickets of intellectual property rights issues that had begun to spring up everywhere, struggling to disentangle tiny shoots of weak, drab good from vibrant, hardy evil, William worked in the garden and on the house. And to earn, as he insisted on doing, a modest living of his own, he proofread for a small company that published books about music. Eventually they rented out the top story of the brownstone, for a purely nominal sum, to Naomi, whom they'd met around the neighborhood and liked. It was nice to come home late and see her light on, to run into her on the stairs.

She'd been just a girl when she'd moved in, really, nodding and smiling and ducking her head when she encountered them at the door or on the way up with intractable brown paper bags, bulging as if they were full of cats but tufted with peculiar groceries—vegetables sprouting globular appendages and sloshing cartons of mysterious liquids. Then, farther along in the distant past, Margaret had appeared.

Where there had been one in the market, at the corner bar, on the stairs, now there were two. Naomi, short and lively, given to boots and charming cowgirl skirts; tall, arrestingly bony Margaret with arched eyebrows and bright red hair. Now there were lines around Naomi's eyes; she had widened and settled downward. One rarely recalled Margaret's early, sylvan loveliness.

So long ago! Though it felt that way only at moments—when Otto passed by a mirror unprepared, or when he bothered to register the probable ages (in comparison with his own) of people whom—so recently!—he would have taken for contemporaries, or when he caught a glimpse of a middle-aged person coming toward him on the street who turned into William. Or sometimes when he thought of Sharon.

And right this moment, Naomi and Margaret were on their way back from China with their baby. The adoption went through! Naomi's recent, ecstatic e-mail had announced. Adoption. Had the girls upstairs failed to notice that they had slid into their late forties?

Sharon's apartment looked, as always, as if it had been sealed up in some innocent period against approaching catastrophes. There were several blond wood chairs, and a sofa, all slipcovered in a nubby, unexceptionable fabric that suggested nuns' sleepwear, and a plastic hassock. The simple, undemanding shapes of the furnishings portrayed the humility of daily life—or at least, Otto thought, of Sharon's daily life. The Formica counter was blankly unstained, and in the cupboards there was a set of heavy, functional, white dishes.

It was just possible, if you craned, and scrunched yourself properly, to glimpse through the window a corner of Sharon's beloved planetarium, where she spent many of her waking hours; the light that made its way to the window around the encircling buildings was pale and tender, an elegy from a distant sun. Sharon herself sometimes seemed to Otto like an apparition from the past. As the rest of them aged, her small frame continued to look like a young girl's; her hair remained an infantine flaxen. To hold it back she wore bright, plastic barrettes.

A large computer, a gift from Otto, sat in the living room, its screen permanently alive. Charts of the constellations were pinned to one of the bedroom walls, and on the facing wall were topographical maps. Peeking into the room, one felt as if one were traveling with Sharon in some zone between earth and sky; yes, down there, so far away—that was our planet.

Why did he need so many things in his life, Otto wondered; why did all these things have to be so special? Special, beautiful plates; special, beautiful furniture; special, beautiful everything. And all that specialness, it occurred to him, intended only to ensure that no one—especially himself—could possibly underestimate his value. Yet it actually served to illustrate how corroded he was, how threadbare his native resources, how impoverished his discourse with everything that lived and was human.

Sharon filled a teakettle with water and lit one of the stove burners. The kettle was dented, but oddly bright, as if she'd just scrubbed it. "I'm thinking of buying a sculpture," she said. "Nothing big. Sit down, Otto, if you'd like. With some pleasant vertical bits."

"Good plan," Otto said. "Where did you find it?"

"Find it?" she said. "Oh. It's a theoretical sculpture. Abstract in that sense, at least. Because I realized you were right."

About what? Well, it was certainly plausible that he had once idly said something about a sculpture, possibly when he'd helped her find the place and move in, decades earlier. She remembered encyclopedically her years of education, pages of print, apparently arbitrary details of their histories. And some trivial incident or phrase from their childhood might at any time fetch up from her mind and flop down in front of her, alive and thrashing.

No, but it couldn't be called "remembering" at all, really, could it? That simply wasn't what people meant by "remembering." No act of mind or the psyche was needed for Sharon to reclaim anything, because nothing in her brain ever sifted down out of precedence. The passage of time failed to distance, blur, or diminish her experiences. The nacreous layers that formed around the events in one's history to smoothe, distinguish, and beautify them never materialized around Sharon's; her history skittered here and there in its original sharp grains on a depthless plane that resembled neither calendar nor clock.

"I just had the most intense episode of déjà vu," William

said, as if Otto's thoughts had sideswiped him. "We were all
sitting here—"

"We *are* all sitting here," Otto said.

"But that's what I mean," William said. "It's supposed to be
some kind of synaptic glitch, isn't it? So you feel as if you've
already had the experience just as you're having it?"

"In the view of many neurologists," Sharon said. "But our
understanding of time is dim. It's patchy. We really don't know
to what degree time is linear, and under what circumstances.
Is it actually, in fact, manifold? Or pleated? Is it frilly? And
what is our relationship to it? Our relationship to it is ex-
tremely problematical."

"I think it's a fine idea for you to have a sculpture," Otto
said. "But I don't consider it a necessity."

Her face was as transparent as a child's. Or at least as hers
had been as a child, reflecting every passing cloud, rippling at
the tiniest disturbance. And her smile! The sheer wattage—no
one over eleven smiled like that. "We're using the teabag-in-
the-cup method," she said. "Greater scope for the exercise of
free will, streamlined technology . . ."

"Oh, goody," William said. "Darjeeling."

Otto stared morosely at his immersed bag and the dark
halo spreading from it. How long would Sharon need them to
stay? When would she want them to go? It was tricky, weav-
ing a course between what might cause her to feel rejected
and what might cause her to feel embattled . . . Actually,
though, how did these things work? Did bits of water escort
bits of tea from the bag, or what? "How is flavor dissemi-
nated?" he said.

"It has to do with oils," Sharon said.

Strange, you really couldn't tell, half the time, whether
someone was knowledgeable or insane. At school Sharon had

shown an astounding talent for the sciences—for everything. For mathematics, especially. Her mind was so rarefied, so crystalline, so adventurous, that none of the rest of them could begin to follow. She soared into graduate school, practically still a child; she was one of the few blessed people, it seemed, whose destiny was clear.

Her professors were astonished by her leaps of thought, by the finesse and elegance of her insights. She arrived at hypotheses by sheer intuition and with what eventually one of her mentors described as an almost alarming speed; she was like a dancer, he said, out in the cosmos springing weightlessly from star to star. Drones, merely brilliant, crawled along behind with laborious proofs that supported her assertions.

A tremendous capacity for metaphor, Otto assumed it was; a tremendous sensitivity to the deep structures of the universe. Uncanny. It seemed no more likely that there would be human beings thus equipped than human beings born with satellite dishes growing out of their heads.

He himself was so literal minded he couldn't understand the simplest scientific or mathematical formulation. Plain old electricity, for example, with its amps and volts and charges and conductivity! Metaphors, presumably—metaphors to describe some ectoplasmic tiger in the walls just spoiling to shoot through the wires the instant the cage door was opened and out into the bulb. And molecules! What on earth were people talking about? If the table was actually just a bunch of swarming motes, bound to one another by nothing more than some amicable commonality of form, then why didn't your teacup go crashing through it?

But from the time she was tiny, Sharon seemed to be in kindly, lighthearted communion with the occult substances that lay far within and far beyond the human body. It was all as easy for her as reading was for him. She was a creature of the universe. As were they all, come to think of it, though so few were privileged to feel it. And how hospitable and correct she'd made the universe seem when she spoke of even its most rococo and farfetched attributes!

The only truly pleasurable moments at the family dinner table were those rare occasions when Sharon would talk. He remembered one evening—she would have been in grade school. She was wearing a red sweater; pink barrettes held back her hair. She was speaking of holes in space—holes in nothing! No, not in nothing, Sharon explained patiently—in space. And the others, older and larger, laid down their speared meat and listened, uncomprehending and entranced, as though to distant, wordless singing.

Perhaps, Otto sometimes consoled himself, they could be forgiven for failing to identify the beginnings. How could the rest of them, with their ordinary intellects, have followed Sharon's rapid and arcane speculations, her penetrating apperceptions, closely enough to identify with any certainty the odd associations and disjunctures that seemed to be showing up in her conversation? In any case, at a certain point as she wandered out among the galaxies, among the whirling particles and ineffable numbers, something leaked in her mind, smudging the text of the cosmos, and she was lost.

Or perhaps, like a lightbulb, she was helplessly receptive to an overwhelming influx. She was so physically delicate, and yet the person to whom she was talking might take a step back. And she, in turn, could be crushed by the slightest shift in someone's expression or tone. It was as if the chemistry of her personality burned off the cushion of air between herself and others. Then one night she called, very late, to alert Otto to a newspaper article about the sorting of lettuces; if he were to give each letter its numerological value . . . The phone cord thrummed with her panic.

When their taxi approached the hospital on that first occasion, Sharon was dank and electric with terror; her skin looked like wet plaster. Otto felt like an assassin as he led her in, and then she was ushered away somewhere. The others joined him in the waiting room, and after several hours had the opportunity to browbeat various doctors into hangdog temporizing. Many people got better, didn't they, had only one episode, didn't they, led fully functioning lives? Why wouldn't Sharon be part of that statistic—she, who was so able, so lively, so sweet—so, in a word, healthy? When would she be all right?

That depended on what they meant by "all right," one of the doctors replied. "We mean by 'all right' what you mean by 'all right,' you squirrelly bastard," Wesley had shouted, empurpling. Martin paced, sizzling and clicking through his teeth, while Otto sat with his head in his hands, but the fateful, brutal, meaningless diagnosis had already been handed down.

"I got a cake," Sharon said. She glanced at Otto. "Oh. Was that appropriate?"

"Utterly," William said.

Appropriate? What if the cake turned out to be decorated with invisible portents and symbols? What if it revealed itself to be invested with power? To be part of the arsenal of small objects—nail scissors, postage stamps, wrapped candies—that lay about in camouflage to fool the credulous doofus like himself just as they were winking their malevolent signals to Sharon?

Or what if the cake was, after all, only an inert teatime treat? A cake required thought, effort, expenditure—all that on a negligible scale for most people, but in Sharon's stripped and cautious life, nothing was negligible. A cake. Wasn't that enough to bring one to one's knees? "Very appropriate," Otto concurred.

"Do you miss the fish?" Sharon said, lifting the cake from its box.

Fish? Otto's heart flipped up, pounding. Oh, the box, fish, nothing.

"We brought them home from the dime store in little cardboard boxes," she explained to William, passing the cake on its plate and a large knife over to him.

"I had a hamster," William said. The cake bulged resiliently around the knife.

"Did it have to rush around on one of those things?" Sharon asked.

"I think it liked to," William said, surprised.

"Let us hope so," Otto said. "Of course it did."

"I loved the castles and the colored sand," Sharon said. "But it was no life for a fish. We had to flush them down the toilet."

William, normally so fastidious about food, appeared to be happily eating his cake, which tasted, to Otto, like landfill. And William had brought Sharon flowers, which it never would have occurred to Otto to do.

Why had lovely William stayed with disagreeable old him for all this time? What could possibly explain his appeal for William, Otto wondered? Certainly not his appearance, nor his musical sensitivity—middling at best—nor, clearly, his temperament. Others might have been swayed by the money that he made so easily, but not William. William cared as little about that as did Otto himself. And yet, through all these years, William had cleaved to him. Or at least, usually. Most of the uncleavings, in fact, had been Otto's—brief, preposterous seizures having to do with God knows what. Well, actually he himself would be the one to know what, wouldn't he, Otto thought. Having to do with—who *did* know what? Oh, with fear, with flight, the usual. A bit of glitter, a mirage, a chimera . . . A lot of commotion just for a glimpse into his own life, the real one—a life more vivid, more truly his, than the one that was daily at hand.

"Was there something you wanted to see me about?" Sharon asked.

"Well, I just . . ." Powerful beams of misery intersected in Otto's heart; was it true? Did he always have a reason when he called Sharon? Did he never drop in just to say hello? Not that anyone ought to "drop in" on Sharon. Or on anyone, actually. How barbarous.

"Your brother's here in an ambassadorial capacity," William said. "I'm just here for the cake."

"Ambassadorial?" Sharon looked alarmed.

"Oh, it's only Thanksgiving," Otto said. "Corinne was hoping— I was hoping—"

"Otto, I can't. I just can't. I don't want to sit there being an exhibit of robust good health, or noncontaminatingness, or the triumph of the human spirit, or whatever it is that Corinne needs me to illustrate. Just tell them everything is okay."

He looked at his cake. William was right. This was terribly unfair. "Well, I don't blame you," he said. "I wouldn't go myself, if I could get out of it."

"If you had a good enough excuse."

"I only—" But of course it was exactly what he had meant; he had meant that Sharon had a good enough excuse. "I'm—"

"Tell Corinne I'm all right."

Otto started to speak again, but stopped.

"Otto, please." Sharon looked at her hands, folded in her lap. "It's all right."

"I've sometimes wondered if it might not be possible, in theory, to remember something that you—I mean the aspect of yourself that you're aware of—haven't experienced yet," William said later. "I mean, we really *don't* know whether time is linear, so—"

"Would you stop that?" Otto said. "*You're* not insane."

"I'm merely speaking theoretically."

"Well, don't! And your memory has nothing to do with whether time is 'really,' whatever you mean by that, linear. It's plenty linear for us! Cradle to grave? Over the hill? It's a one-way street, my dear. My hair is not sometimes there and sometimes not there; we're *not* getting any younger."

At moments it occurred to Otto that what explained his appeal for William was the fact that they lived in the same apartment. That William was idiotically accepting, idiotically pliant. Perhaps William was so deficient in subtlety, so insensitive to nuance, that he simply couldn't tell the difference between Otto and anyone else. "And, William—I wish you'd get back to your tennis."

"It's a bore. Besides, you didn't want me playing with Jason, as I remember."

"Well, I was out of my mind. And at this point it's your arteries I worry about."

"You know," William said and put his graceful hand on Otto's arm. "I don't think she's any more unhappy than the rest of us, really, most of the time. That smile! I mean, that smile can't come out of nowhere."

There actually were no children to speak of. Corinne and Wesley's "boys" put in a brief, unnerving appearance. When last seen, they had been surly, furtive, persecuted-looking, snickering, hulking, hairy adolescents, and now here they were, having undergone the miraculous transformation. How gratified Wesley must be! They had shed their egalitarian denim chrysalis and had risen up in the crisp, mean mantle of their class.

The older one even had a wife, whom Corinne treated with a stricken, fluttery deference as if she were a suitcase full of weapons-grade plutonium. The younger one was restlessly on his own. When, early in the evening the three stood and announced to Corinne with thuggish placidity that they were about to leave ("I'm afraid we've got to shove off now, Ma"), Otto jumped to his feet. As he allowed his hand to be crushed, he felt the relief of a mayor watching an occupying power depart his city.

Martin's first squadron of children (Maureen's) weren't even mentioned. Who knew what army of relatives, step-relatives, half-relatives they were reinforcing by now. But there were—Otto shuddered faintly—Martin's two newest (Laurie's). Yes, just as Corinne had said, they, too, were growing up. Previously indistinguishable wads of self-interest, they had developed perceptible features—maybe even characteristics; it appeared reasonable, after all, that they had been given names.

What on earth was it that William did to get children to converse? Whenever Otto tried to have a civilized encounter with a child, the child just stood there with its finger in its nose. But Martin's two boys were chattering away, showing off to William their whole heap of tiresome electronics.

William was frowning with interest. He poked at a keyboard, which sent up a shower of festive little beeps, and the boys flung themselves at him, cheering, while Laurie smiled meltingly. How times had changed. Not so many years earlier, such a tableau would have had handcuffs rattling in the wings.

The only other representative of "the children" to whom Corinne had referred with such pathos, was Martin's daughter, Portia (Viola's). She'd been hardly more than a toddler at last sight, though she now appeared to be about—what? Well, anyhow, a little girl. "What are the domestic arrangements?" Otto asked. "Is she living with Martin and Laurie these days, or is she with her mother?"

"That crazy Viola has gone back to England, thank God; Martin has de facto custody."

"Speaking of Martin, where is he?"

"I don't ask," Corinne said.

Otto waited.

"I don't ask," Corinne said again. "And if Laurie wants to share, she'll tell you herself."

"Is Martin in the pokey already?" Otto asked.

"This is not a joke, Otto. I'm sorry to tell you that Martin has been having an affair with some girl."

"Again?"

Corinne stalled, elaborately adjusting her bracelet. "I'm sorry to tell you she's his trainer."

"His *trainer*? How can Martin have a trainer? If Martin has a trainer, what can explain Martin's body?"

"Otto, it's not funny," Corinne said with ominous primness. "The fact is, Martin has been looking very good, lately. But of course you wouldn't have seen him."

All those wives—and a trainer! How? Why would any woman put up with Martin? Martin, who always used to eat his dessert so slowly that the rest of them had been made to wait, squirming at the table, watching as he took his voluptuous, showy bites of chocolate cake or floating island long after they'd finished their own.

"I'm afraid it's having consequences for Portia. Do you see what she's doing?"

"She's—" Otto squinted over at Portia. "What is she doing?"

"Portia, come here, darling," Corinne called.

Portia looked at them for a moment, then wandered sedately over. "And now we'll have a word with Aunt Corinne," she said to her fist as she approached. "Hello, Aunt Corinne."

"Portia," Corinne said, "do you remember Uncle Otto?"

"And Uncle Otto," Portia added to her fist. She regarded him with a clear, even gaze. In its glade of light and silence they encountered one another serenely. She held out her fist to him. "Would you tell our listeners what you do when you go to work, Uncle Otto?"

"Well," Otto said, to Portia's fist, "first I take the elevator up to the twentieth floor, and then I sit down at my desk, and then I send Bryan out for coffee and a bagel—"

"Otto," Corinne said, "Portia is trying to learn what it is you *do*. Something I'm sure we'd all like to know."

"Oh," Otto said. "Well, I'm a lawyer, dear. Do you know what that is?"

"Otto," Corinne said wearily, "Portia's father is a lawyer."

"Portia's father is a global-money mouthpiece!" Otto said.

"Aunt Corinne is annoyed," Portia commented to her fist. "Now Uncle Otto and Aunt Corinne are looking at your correspondent. Now they're not."

"Tell me, Portia," Otto said; the question had sprung insistently into his mind, "what are you going to be when you grow up?"

Her gaze was strangely relaxing. "You know, Uncle Otto," she said pensively to her fist, "people used to ask me that a lot."

Huh! Yes, that was probably something people asked only very small children, when speculation would be exclusively a matter of amusing fantasy. "Well, I was only just mulling it over," Otto said.

"Portia, darling," Corinne said, "why don't you run into the kitchen and do a cooking segment with Bea and Cleveland?"

"It's incredible," Otto said when Portia disappeared, "she looks exactly like Sharon did at that age."

"Ridiculous," Corinne said. "She takes after her father."

Martin? Stuffy, venal Martin, with his nervous eyes and scoopy nose, and squashy head balanced on his shirt collar? Portia's large, gray eyes, the flaxen hair, the slightly oversized ears and fragile neck recapitulated absolutely Sharon's appearance in this child who probably wouldn't remember ever having seen Sharon. "Her *father*?"

"Her father," Corinne said. "Martin. Portia's father."

"I know Martin is her father. I just can't divine the resemblance."

"Well, there's certainly no resemblance to— Wesley—" Corinne called over to him. "Must you read the newspaper? This is a social occasion. Otto, will you listen, please? I'm trying to tell you something. The truth is, we're all quite worried about Portia."

Amazing how fast one's body reacted. Fear had vacuumed the blood right through his extremities. One's body, the primeval parts of one's brain—how fast they were! Much faster than that recent part with the words and thoughts and so on, what was it? The cortex, was that it? He'd have to ask William, he thought, his blood settling back down. That sort of wrinkly stuff on top that looked like crumpled wrapping paper.

"Laurie is worried sick. The truth is, that's one reason I was so anxious for you to join us today. I wanted your opinion on the matter."

"On what matter?" Otto said. "I have no idea what this is about. She's fine. She seems fine. She's just playing."

"I know she's just playing, Otto. It's *what* she's playing that concerns me."

"What she's playing? What is she playing? She's playing radio, or something! Is that so sinister? The little boys seem to be playing something called Hammer Her Flat."

"I'm sure not. Oh, gracious. You and Sharon were both so right not to have children."

"Excuse me?" Otto said incredulously.

"It's not the radio aspect per se that I'm talking about, it's what that represents. The child is an observer. She sees herself as an outsider. As alienated."

"There's nothing wrong with being observant. Other members of this family could benefit from a little of that quality."

"She can't relate directly to people."

"Who can?" Otto said.

"Half the time Viola doesn't even remember the child is alive! You watch. She won't send Portia a Christmas present. She probably won't even call. Otto, listen. We've always said that Viola is 'unstable,' but, frankly, Viola is *psychotic*. Do you understand what I'm saying to you? Portia's *mother*, Otto. It's just as you were saying, *there's a geneti—*"

"I was saying *what*? I was saying nothing! I was only saying—"

"Oh, dear!" Laurie exclaimed. She had an arm around Portia, who was crying.

"What in hell is going on now?" Wesley demanded, slamming down his newspaper.

"I'm afraid Bea and Cleveland may have said something to her," Laurie said, apologetically.

"Oh, terrific," Wesley said. "Now I know what I'm paying them for."

"It's all right, sweetie," Laurie said. "It all happened a long time ago."

"But why are we celebrating that we killed them?" Portia asked, and started crying afresh.

"We're not celebrating because we killed the Indians, darling," Laurie said. "We're celebrating because we ate dinner with them."

"Portia still believes in Indians!" one of the little boys exclaimed.

"So do we all, Josh," Wesley said. "They live at the North Pole and make toys for good little—"

"Wesley, please!" Corinne said.

"Listener poll," Portia said to her fist. "Did we eat dinner with the Indians, or did we kill them?" She strode over to Otto and held out her fist.

"We ate dinner with them and *then* we killed them," Otto realized, out loud to his surprise.

"Who are you to slag off Thanksgiving, old boy?" Wesley said. "You're wearing a fucking bow tie."

"So are you, for that matter," Otto said, awkwardly embracing Portia, who was crying again.

"And *I* stand behind my tie," Wesley said, rippling upward from his chair.

"It was Portia's birthday last week!" Laurie interrupted loudly, and Wesley sank back down. "Wasn't it!"

Portia nodded, gulping, and wiped at her tears.

"How old are you now, Portia?" William asked.

"Nine," Portia said.

"That's great," William said. "Get any good stuff?"

Portia nodded again.

"And Portia's mommy sent a terrific present, didn't she," Laurie said.

"Oh, what was it, sweetie?" Corinne said.

Laurie turned pink and her head seemed to flare out slightly in various directions. "You don't have to say, darling, if you don't like."

Portia held on to the arm of Otto's chair and swung her leg aimlessly back and forth. "My mother gave me two tickets to go to Glyndebourne on my eighteenth birthday," she said in a tiny voice.

Wesley snorted. "Got your frock all picked out, Portia?"

"I won't be going to Glyndebourne, Uncle Wesley," Portia said with dignity.

There was a sudden silence in the room.

"Why not, dear?" Otto asked. He was trembling, he noticed.

Portia looked out at all of them. Tears still clung to her face. "Because." She raised her fist to her mouth again. "Factoid: According to the Mayan calendar, the world is going to end in the year 2012, the year before this reporter's eighteenth birthday."

"All right," Corinne whispered to Otto. "Now do you see?"

"You're right, as always," Otto said, in the taxi later, "they're no worse than anyone else's. They're all awful. I really don't see the point in it. Just think! Garden garden garden garden garden, two happy people, and it could have gone on forever! They knew, they'd been told, but they ate it anyway, and from there on out, *family*! Shame, fear, jobs, mortality, envy, murder . . ."

"Well," William said brightly, "and sex."

"There's that," Otto conceded.

"In fact, you could look at both family and mortality simply as by-products of sexual reproduction."

"I don't really see the point of sexual reproduction, either," Otto said. "*I* wouldn't stoop to it."

"Actually, that's very interesting, you know; they think that the purpose of sexual reproduction is to purge the genome of harmful mutations. Of course, they also seem to think it isn't working."

"Then why not scrap it?" Otto said. "Why not let us divide again, like our dignified and immortal forebear, the amoeba."

William frowned. "I'm not really sure that—"

"Joke," Otto said.

"Oh, yes. Well, but I suppose sexual reproduction is fairly entrenched by now—people aren't going to give it up without a struggle. And besides, family confers certain advantages as a social unit, doesn't it."

"No. What advantages?"

"Oh, rudimentary education. Protection."

" 'Education'! Ha! 'Protection'! Ha!"

"Besides," William said. "It's broadening. You meet people in your family you'd never happen to run into otherwise. And anyhow, obviously the desire for children is hardwired."

" 'Hardwired.' You know, that's a term I've really come to loathe! It explains nothing, it justifies anything; you might as well say, 'Humans have children because the Great Moth in the Sky wants them to.' Or, 'Humans have children because humans have children.' 'Hardwired,' please! It's lazy, it's specious, it's perfunctory, and it's utterly without depth."

"Why does it have to have depth?" William said. "It *refers* to depth. It's good, clean science."

"It's not science at all, it's a cliché. It's a redundancy."

"Otto, why do you always scoff at me when I raise a scientific point?"

"I don't! I don't scoff at you. I certainly don't mean to. It's just that this particular phrase, used in this particular way, isn't very interesting. I mean, you're telling me that something is biologically *inherent* in human experience, but you're not telling me anything *about* human experience."

"I wasn't intending to," William said. "I wasn't trying to. If you want to talk about human experience, then let's talk about it."

"All right," Otto said. It was painful, of course, to see William irritated, but almost a relief to know that it could actually happen. "Let's, then. By all means."

"So?"

"Well?"

"Any particular issues?" William said. "Any questions?"

Any! *Billions*. But that was always just the problem: how to disentangle one; how to pluck it up and clothe it in presentable words? Otto stared, concentrating. Questions were roiling in the pit of his mind like serpents, now a head rising up from the seething mass, now a rattling tail . . . He closed his eyes. If only he could get his brain to relax . . . Relax, relax . . . Relax, relax, relax . . . "Oh, you know, William—is there anything at home to eat? Believe it or not, I'm starving again."

————

There was absolutely no reason to fear that Portia would have anything other than an adequately happy, adequately fruitful life. No reason at all. Oh, how prudent of Sharon not to have come yesterday. Though in any case, she had been as present to the rest of them as if she had been sitting on the sofa. And the rest of them had probably been as present to her as she had been to them.

When one contemplated Portia, when one contemplated Sharon, when one contemplated one's own apparently pointless, utterly trivial being, the questions hung all around one, as urgent as knives at the throat. But the instant one tried to grasp one of them and turn it to one's own purpose and pierce through the murk, it became as blunt and useless as a piece of cardboard.

All one could dredge up were platitudes: one comes into the world alone, snore snore; one, snore snore, departs the world alone . . .

What would William have to say? Well, it was a wonderful thing to live with an inquiring and mentally active person; no one could quarrel with that. William was immaculate in his intentions, unflagging in his efforts. But what drove one simply insane was the vagueness. Or, really, the banality. Not that it was William's job to explicate the foggy assumptions of one's culture, but one's own ineptitude was galling enough; one hardly needed to consult a vacuity expert!

And how could one think at all, or even just casually ruminate, with William practicing, as he had been doing since they'd awakened. Otto had forgotten what a strain it all was—even without any exasperating social nonsense—those few days preceding the concert; you couldn't think, you couldn't concentrate on the newspaper. You couldn't even really hear the phone, which seemed to be ringing now—

Nor could you make any sense of what the person on the other end of it might be saying. "What?" Otto shouted into it. "You what?"

Could he—the phone cackled into the lush sheaves of William's arpeggios—*bribery, sordid out*—

"William!" Otto yelled. "Excuse me? Could I what?"

The phone cackled some more. "Excuse me," Otto said. *"William!"*

The violin went quiet. "Excuse me?" Otto said again into the phone, which was continuing to emit jibberish. "Sort *what* out? Took her *where* from the library?"

"I'm trying to explain, sir," the phone said. "I'm calling from the hospital."

"She was *taken* from the library *by force*?"

"Unfortunately, sir, as I've tried to explain, she was understood to be homeless."

"And so she was taken away? By force? That could be construed as kidnapping, you know."

"I'm only reporting what the records indicate, sir. The records do not indicate that your sister was kidnapped."

"I don't understand. Is it a crime to be homeless?"

"Apparently your sister did not claim to be homeless. Apparently your sister claimed to rent an apartment. Is this not the case? Is your sister in fact homeless?"

"My sister is not homeless! My sister rents an apartment! Is that a crime? What does this have to do with why my sister was taken away, by force, from the library?"

"Sir, I'm calling from the hospital."

"I'm a taxpayer!" Otto shouted. William was standing in the doorway, violin in one hand, bow in the other, watching gravely. "I'm a lawyer! Why is information being withheld from me?"

"Information is not being withheld from you, sir, please! I understand that you are experiencing concern, and I'm trying to explain this situation in a way that you will understand what has occurred. It is a policy that homeless people tend to congregate in the library, using the restrooms, and some of these people may be removed, if, for example, these people exhibit behaviors that are perceived to present a potential danger."

"Are you *reading* this from something? Is it a crime to use a *public bathroom?*"

"When people who do not appear to have homes to go to, appear to be confused and disoriented—"

"Is it a *crime* to be *confused?*"

"Please calm *down*, sir. The evaluation was not ours. What I'm trying to tell you is that according to the report, your sister became obstreperous when she was brought to the homeless shelter. She appeared to be disoriented. She did not appear to understand why she was being taken to the homeless shelter."

"Shall I go with you?" William said, when Otto put down the phone.

"No," Otto said. "Stay, please. Practice."

So, once again. Waiting in the dingy whiteness, the fearsome whiteness no doubt of heaven, heaven's sensible shoes, overtaxed heaven's obtuse smiles and ruthless tranquillity, heaven's asphyxiating clouds dropped over the screams bleeding faintly from behind closed doors. He waited in a room with others too dazed even to note the television that hissed and bristled in front of them or to turn the pages of the sticky, dog-eared magazines they held, from which they could have learned how to be happy, wealthy, and sexually appealing; they waited, like Otto, to learn instead what it was that destiny had already handed down: bad, not that bad, very, very bad.

The doctor, to whom Otto was eventually conducted through the elderly bowels of the hospital, looked like an epic hero—shining, arrogant, supple. "She'll be fine, now," he said. "You'll be fine now, won't you?"

Sharon's smile, the sudden birth of a little sun, and the doctor's own brilliant smile met, and ignited for an instant. Otto felt as though a missile had exploded in his chest.

"Don't try biting any of those guys from the city again," the doctor said, giving Sharon's childishly rounded, childishly humble, shoulder a companionable pat. "They're poisonous."

"Bite them!" Otto exclaimed, admiration leaping up in him like a dog at a chain link fence, on the other side of which a team of uniformed men rushed at his defenseless sister with clubs.

"I did?" Sharon cast a repentant, sidelong glance at the doctor.

The doctor shrugged and flipped back his blue-black hair, dislodging sparkles of handsomeness. "The file certainly painted an unflattering portrait of your behavior. 'Menaced dentally,' it says, or something of the sort. Now, listen. Take care of yourself. Follow Dr. Shiga's instructions. Because I don't want to be seeing you around here, okay?"

He and Sharon looked at each other for a moment, then traded a little, level, intimate smile. "It's okay with me," she said.

Otto took Sharon to a coffee shop near her apartment and bought her two portions of macaroni and cheese.

"How was it?" she said. "How was everyone?"

"Thanksgiving? Oh. You didn't miss much."

She put down her fork. "Aren't you going to have anything, Otto?"

"I'll have something later with William," he said.

"Oh," she said. She sat very still. "Of course."

He was a monster. Well, no one was perfect. But in any case, her attention returned to her macaroni. Not surprising that she was ravenous. How long had her adventures lasted? Her clothing was rumpled and filthy.

"I didn't know you liked the library," he said.

"Don't think I'm not grateful for the computer," she said. "It was down."

He nodded, and didn't press her.

There was a bottle of wine breathing on the table, and William had managed to maneuver dinner out of the mysterious little containers and the limp bits of organic matter from the fridge, which Otto had inspected earlier in a doleful search for lunch. "Bad?" William asked.

"Fairly," Otto said.

"Want to tell me?" William said.

Otto gestured impatiently. "Oh, what's the point."

"Okay," William said. "Mustard with that? It's good."

"I can't stand it that she has to live like this!" Otto said.

William shook his head. "Everyone is so alone," he said.

Otto yelped.

"What?" William said. "What did I do?"

"Nothing," Otto said. He stood, trying to control his trembling. "I'm going to my study. You go on upstairs when you get tired."

"Otto?"

"Just—please."

He sat downstairs in his study with a book in his hand, listening while William rinsed the dishes and put them in the dishwasher, and went, finally, upstairs. For some time, footsteps persisted oppressively in the bedroom overhead. When they ceased, Otto exhaled with relief.

A pale tincture spread into the study window; the pinched little winter sun was rising over the earth, above the neighbors' buildings. Otto listened while William came down and made himself breakfast, then returned upstairs to practice once again.

The day loomed heavily in front of Otto, like an opponent judging the moment to strike. How awful everything was. How awful he was. How bestial he had been to William; William, who deserved only kindness, only gratitude.

And yet the very thought of glimpsing that innocent face was intolerable. It had been a vastly unpleasant night in the chair, and it would be hours, he knew, before he'd be able to manage an apology without more denunciations leaping from his treacherous mouth.

Hours seemed to be passing, in fact. Or maybe it was minutes. The clock said seven, said ten, said twelve, said twelve, said twelve, seemed to be delirious. Fortunately there were leftovers in the fridge.

Well, if time was the multiplicity Sharon and William seemed to believe it was, maybe it contained multiple Sharons, perhaps some existing in happier conditions, before the tracks diverged, one set leading up into the stars, the other down to the hospital. Otto's mind wandered here and there amid the dimensions, catching glimpses of her skirt, her hair, her hand, as she slipped through the mirrors. Did things have to proceed for each of the Sharons in just exactly the same way?

Did each one grieve for the Olympian destiny that ought to have been hers? Did each grieve for an ordinary life—a life full of ordinary pleasures and troubles—children, jobs, lovers?

Everyone is so alone. For this, all the precious Sharons had to flounder through their loops and tucks of eternity; for this, the shutters were drawn on their aerial and light-filled minds. Each and every Sharon, thrashing through the razor-edged days only in order to be absorbed by this spongy platitude: *everyone is so alone!* Great God, how could it be endured? All the Sharons, for ever and ever, discarded in a phrase.

And those Ottos, sprinkled through the zones of actuality— What were the others doing now? The goldfish gliding, gliding, within the severe perimeter of water; William pausing to introduce himself . . .

Yes, so of course one felt incomplete; of course one felt obstructed and blind. And perhaps every creature on earth, on all the earths, was straining at the obdurate membranes to reunite as its own original entity, the spark of unique consciousness allocated to each being, only then to be irreconcilably refracted through world after world by the prism of time. No wonder one tended to feel so fragile. It was infuriating enough just trying to have contact with a few other people, let alone with all of one's selves!

To think there could be an infinitude of selves, and not an iota of latitude for any of them! An infinitude of Ottos, lugging around that personality, those circumstances, that appearance. Not only once dreary and pointless, but infinitely so.

Oh, was there no escape? Perhaps if one could only concentrate hard enough they could be collected, all those errant, enslaved selves. And in the triumphant instant of their reunification, purified to an unmarked essence, the suffocating Otto-costumes dissolving, a true freedom at last. Oh, how tired he was! But why not make the monumental effort?

Because Naomi and Margaret were arriving at nine to show off this baby of theirs, that was why not.

But anyhow, what on earth was he thinking?

Still, at least he could apologize to William. He was himself, but at least he could go fling that inadequate self at William's feet!

No. At the *very* least he could let poor, deserving William practice undisturbed. He'd wait—patiently, patiently—and when William was finished, William would come downstairs. Then Otto could apologize abjectly, spread every bit of his worthless being at William's feet, comfort him and be comforted, reassure him and be reassured . . .

At a few minutes before nine, William appeared, whistling.

Whistling! "Good practice session?" Otto said. His voice came out cracked, as if it had been hurled against the high prison walls of himself.

"Terrific," William said, and kissed him lightly on the forehead.

Otto opened his mouth. "You know—" he said.

"Oh, listen—" William said. "There really is a baby!" And faintly interspersed among Naomi and Margaret's familiar creakings and bumpings in the hall Otto heard little chirps and gurgles.

"Hello, hello!" William cried, flinging open the door. "Look, isn't she fabulous?"

"We think so," Naomi said, her smile renewing and renewing itself. "Well, she is."

"I can't see if you do that," Margaret said, disengaging the earpiece of her glasses and a clump of her red, crimpy hair from the baby's fist as she attempted to transfer the baby over to William.

"Here." Naomi held out a bottle of champagne. "Take this, too. Well, but you can't keep the baby. Wow, look, she's fascinated by Margaret's hair. I mean, who isn't?"

Otto wasn't, despite his strong feelings about hair in general. "Should we open this up and drink it?" he said, his voice a mechanical voice, his hand a mechanical hand accepting the bottle.

"That was the idea," Naomi said. She blinked up at Otto, smiling hopefully, and rocking slightly from heel to toe.

"Sit. Sit everyone," William said. "Oh, she's sensational!"

Otto turned away to open the champagne and pour it into the lovely glasses somebody or another had given to them sometime or another.

"Well, cheers," William said. "Congratulations. And here's to—"

"Molly," Margaret said. "We decided to keep it simple."

"We figured she's got so much working against her already," Naomi said, "including a couple of geriatric moms with a different ethnicity, and God only knows what infant memories, or whatever you call that stuff you don't remember. We figured we'd name her something nice, that didn't set up all kinds of expectations. Just a nice, friendly, pretty name. And she can take it from there."

"She'll be taking it from there in any case," Otto said, grimly.

The others looked at him.

"I love Maggie," Naomi said. "I always wanted a Maggie, but Margaret said—"

"Well." Margaret shrugged. "I mean—"

"No, I know," Naomi said. "But."

Margaret rolled a little white quilt out on the rug. Plunked down on it, the baby sat, wobbling, with an expression of surprise.

"Look at her!" William said.

"Here's hoping," Margaret said, raising her glass.

So, marvelous. Humans were born, they lived. They glued themselves together in little clumps, and then they died. It was no more, as William had once cheerfully explained, than a way for genes to perpetuate themselves. "The selfish gene," he'd said, quoting, probably detrimentally, someone; you were put on earth to fight for your DNA.

Let the organisms chat. Let them talk. Their voices were as empty as the tinklings of a player-piano. Let the organisms talk about this and that; it was what (as William had so trenchantly pointed out) this particular carbon-based life form did, just as its cousin (according to William) the roundworm romped ecstatically beneath the surface of the planet.

He tried to intercept the baby's glossy, blurry stare. The baby was actually attractive, for a baby, and not bald at all, as it happened. Hello, Otto thought to it, let's you and I communicate in some manner far superior to the verbal one.

The baby ignored him. Whatever she was making of the blanket, the table legs, the shod sets of feet, she wasn't about to let on to Otto. Well, see if he cared.

William was looking at him. So, what was he supposed to do? Oh, all right, he'd contribute. Despite his current clarity of mind.

"And how was China?" he asked. "Was the food as bad as they say?"

Naomi looked at him blankly. "Well, I don't know, actually," she said. "Honey, how was the food?"

"The food," Margaret said. "Not memorable, apparently."

"The things people have to do in order to have children," Otto said.

"We toyed with the idea of giving birth," Margaret said. "That is, Naomi toyed with it."

"At first," Naomi said, "I thought, what a shame to miss an experience that nature intended for us. And, I mean, there was this guy at work, or of course there's always— But then I thought, what, am I an idiot? I mean, just because you've got arms and legs, it doesn't mean you have to—"

"No," William said. "But still. I can understand how you felt."

"Have to what?" Margaret said.

"I can't," Otto said.

"Have to what?" Margaret said.

"I *can't* understand it," Otto said. "I've just never envied the capacity. Others are awestruck, not I. I've never even remotely wished I were able to give birth, and, in fact, I've never wanted a baby. Of course it's inhuman not to want one, but I'm just not human. I'm not a human being. William is a human being. Maybe William wanted a baby. I never thought to ask. Was that what you were trying to tell me the other day, William? Were you trying to tell me that I've ruined your life? *Did* you want a baby? *Have* I ruined your life? Well, it's too bad. I'm sorry. I was too selfish ever to ask if you wanted one, and I'm too selfish to want one myself. I'm more selfish than my own genes. I'm not fighting *for* my DNA, I'm fighting against it!"

"I'm happy as I am," William said. He sat, his arms wrapped tightly around himself, looking at the floor. The baby coughed. "Who needs more champagne?"

"You see?" Otto said into the tundra of silence William

left behind him as he retreated into the kitchen. "I really am a monster."

Miles away, Naomi sat blushing, her hands clasped in her lap. Then she scooped up the baby. "There, there," she said.

But Margaret sat back, eyebrows raised in semicircles, contemplating something that seemed to be hanging a few feet under the ceiling. "Oh, I don't know," she said, and the room shuttled back into proportion. "I suppose you could say it's human to want a child, in the sense that it's biologically mandated. But I mean, you could say that, or you could say it's simply unimaginative. Or you could say it's unselfish or you could say it's selfish, or you could say pretty much anything about it at all. Or you could just say, well, I want one. But when you get right down to it, really, one what? Because, actually—I mean, well, look at Molly. I mean, actually, they're awfully specific."

"I suppose I meant, like, crawl around on all fours, or something," Naomi said. "I mean, just because you've got— But look, there they already are, all these babies, so many of them, just waiting, waiting, waiting on the shelves for someone to take care of them. We could have gone to Romania, we could have gone to Guatemala, we could have gone almost anywhere—just, for various reasons, we decided to go to China."

"And we both really liked the idea," Margaret said, "that you could go as far away as you could possibly get, and there would be your child."

"Uh-huh," Naomi nodded, soberly. "How crazy is that?"

"I abase myself," Otto told William as they washed and dried the champagne glasses. "I don't need to tell you how deeply

I'll regret having embarrassed you in front of Naomi and Margaret." He clasped the limp dishtowel to his heart. "How deeply I'll regret having been insufficiently mawkish about the miracle of life. I don't need to tell you how ashamed I'll feel the minute I calm down. How deeply I'll regret having trampled your life, and how deeply I'll regret being what I am. Well, that last part I regret already. I profoundly regret every tiny crumb of myself. I don't need to go into it all once again, I'm sure. Just send back the form, pertinent boxes checked: 'I intend to accept your forthcoming apology for—' "

"Please stop," William said.

"Oh, how awful to have ruined the life of such a marvelous man! Have I ruined your life? You can tell me; we're friends."

"Otto, I'm going upstairs now. I didn't sleep well last night, and I'm tired."

"Yes, go upstairs."

"Good night," William said.

"Yes, go to sleep, why not?" Oh, it was like trying to pick a fight with a dog toy! "Just you go on off to sleep."

"Otto, listen to me. My concert is tomorrow. I want to be able to play adequately. I don't know why you're unhappy. You do interesting work, you're admired, we live in a wonderful place, we have wonderful friends. We have everything we need and most of the things we want. We have excellent lives by anyone's standard. I'm happy, and I wish you were. I know that you've been upset these last few days, I asked if you wanted to talk, and you said you didn't. Now you do, but this happens to be the one night of the year when I most need my sleep. Can it wait till tomorrow? I'm very tired, and you're obviously very tired, as well. Try and get some sleep, please."

" 'Try *and* get some sleep?' 'Try *and* get some sleep?' This is unbearable! I've spent the best years of my life with a man who doesn't know how to use the word 'and'! 'And' is not part of the infinitive! 'And' means '*in addition to.*' It's not 'Try *and* get some sleep,' it's 'Try *to* get some sleep.' *To! To! To! To! To! To! To! Please try to get some sleep!*"

Otto sat down heavily at the kitchen table and began to sob.

How arbitrary it all was, and cruel. This identity, that identity: Otto, William, Portia, Molly, the doctor . . .

She'd be up now, sitting at her own kitchen table, the white enamel table with a cup of tea, thinking about something, about numbers streaming past in stately sequences, about remote astral pageants . . . The doctor had rested his hand kindly on her shoulder. And what she must have felt then! Oh, to convert that weight of the world's compassion into something worthwhile—the taste, if only she could have lifted his hand and kissed it, the living satin feel of his skin . . . Everyone had to put things aside, to put things aside for good.

The way they had smiled at one another, she and that doctor! What can you do, their smiles had said. The handsome doctor in his handsome-doctor suit and Sharon in her disheveled-lunatic suit; what a charade. In this life, Sharon's little spark of consciousness would be costumed inescapably as a waif at the margins of mental organization and the doctor's would be costumed inescapably as a flashing exemplar of supreme competence; in this life (and, frankly, there would be no other) the hospital was where they would meet.

"Otto—"

A hand was resting on Otto's shoulder.

"William," Otto said. It was William. They were in the clean, dim kitchen. The full moon had risen high over the neighbors' buildings, where the lights were almost all out. Had he been asleep? He blinked up at William, whose face, shadowed against the light of the night sky, was as inflected, as ample in mystery as the face in the moon. "It's late, my darling," Otto said. "I'm tired. What are we doing down here?"

LIKE IT OR NOT

Kate would have a little tour of the coast, Giovanna would have the satisfaction of having provided an excursion for her American houseguest without having to interrupt her own work, and the man whom everyone called Harry would have the pleasure, as Giovanna put it, of Kate's company: demonstrably a good thing for all concerned.

"I wish this weren't happening," Kate said. "I'll be inconveniencing him. And besides—"

"No." Giovanna waved a finger. "This is the point. He goes every few months to check on this place of his. He loves to show people about, he loves to poke around the little shops. So, why not? You'll go with him as far as one of the towns, you'll give him a chance to shop, you'll give him a chance to shine, you'll spend the night at some pleasant hotel, then he'll go on and you'll find your way back here by taxi and train."

So, yes—it was hard to say just who was doing whom a favor . . .

"The coast is very beautiful," Giovanna added. "You don't feel like enjoying such things right now, I know, but right now is when your chance presents itself."

The whole thing had twisted itself into shape several days earlier at a party—a noisy roomful of Giovanna's friends.

Harry had been speaking to Kate in English, but his unplaceable accent and the wedges of other languages flashing around Kate chopped up her concentration. She tried to follow his voice—he was obliged to go frequently to the coast . . .

Had she left enough in the freezer? Brice and Blair were hardly children, but whenever they came back home they reverted to sheer incompetence. Besides, they'd be so busy dealing with their father . . .

And was Kate fond of it? the person, Harry, was asking.

"Fond of . . ." She searched his face. "Oh. Well, actually I've never . . ." and then both she and he were silenced, rounding this corner of the conversation and seeing its direction.

Giovanna had simply stood there, smiling a bright, vague smile, as though she couldn't hear a thing. And Harry had been polite—technically, at least; Kate gave him every opportunity to weasel out of an invitation to her, but he'd shouldered the burden manfully. And so there it was, the thing that was going to happen, like it or not. Still, Giovanna was right. And perhaps the very fact that Kate was in no mood to do anything proved, in fact, that she should submit gracefully to whatever . . . *opportunity* came her way.

Over and over, now that she was visiting Giovanna, she'd recall—the phone ringing, herself answering . . . as if, listening hard enough this time, she might hear something different. Sitting on the sofa, shoes off . . . It was December 3, the date was on the quizzes she was grading. She'd almost knocked over her cup of tea, answering the phone with her hands full of papers. "Has Baker talked to you about what's going on with him?" Norman had asked.

It was the gentleness of Norman's voice that stayed with

her, the tea swaying in her cup. What practical difference did Baker's illness make to her life? Almost none. It was a good fifteen years since she and Baker had gotten divorced.

She'd sent out her annual Christmas letter:

Sorry to be late this year, everyone, (as usual!) but school seems to get more and more time-consuming. Always more administrative annoyances, more student crises . . . This year we had to learn a new drill, in addition to the fire drill and the cyclone drill—a drive-by shooting drill! You can tell how old all the teachers here are by what we do when that bell goes off. Anyone else remember the atomic-bomb drill? Whenever the alarm rings I still just dive under the desk. Blair is surviving her first year of law school. Brice swears he'll never . . .

and so on. She looked at what she'd written—apparently a description of her life.

To Giovanna's copy she appended a note: "I'm fine, really, but Baker's sick. Very. And Blair and Brice are here this week spending days with him and Norman, nights with me. Blair's fiancé calls every few hours, frantically apologizing. He pleads, she storms. Grand opera! Will she just please tell him why she's angry? She's not angry, she insists—it's just all this *apologizing* . . . I guess the diva-gene skipped a generation. Speaking of which, Mother asks after you. She still talks about how that boring friend of Baker's followed you back to Europe after the wedding. She's weirdly sweet sometimes these days. Think that means she's dying? It scares me out of my wits, actually . . ."

Giovanna faxed Kate at school: Come stay over spring break. No excuses.

It had been so many years since they'd seen each other, letters were so rarely exchanged, that Giovanna had come to seem abstract; Kate hadn't even been aware of confiding. She stared at the fax as she went into her classroom. The map was still rolled down over the blackboard from the previous class. In fact, Giovanna was· not only capable, evidently, of reading the note, she was also less than fifteen inches away.

They had met almost thirty years earlier at a college to which Kate had been sent for its patrician reputation and its august location, and to which Giovanna had been exiled for its puritanical reputation and backwater location, far removed from her own country and her customary amusements. Kate had first encountered the famous Giovanna in the hall outside her room, passed out on the floor, had dragged her inside, revived her, and from then on had joyfully assisted her in and out windows on extralegal forays, after hours, to destinations unequivocally off-limits, with scandalously older men—the more distinguished of the professors, local politicians, visiting lecturers and entertainers . . .

The two girls found one anothers' characteristics, both national and personal, hilarious and illuminating. They scrutinized each other—the one stolid, socially awkward, midwestern, and oblique; the other polished, European, and satirical—as if each were looking into a transforming mirror, which reflected now certain qualities, now certain others. So many possibilities had floated in that mirror!

While Giovanna worked long hours at her firm, Kate walked dutifully through the city, staring at churches, paintings, and fountains. What had she seen? She couldn't have said. She drew the line absolutely, she'd told Blair, at taking photographs. "But, Mother," Blair had said. "You'd get so much more out of your trip!" Poor Brice—how would he be faring at home with his sister? All his life Blair had been trying to turn him upside down and shake him, as if she could dislodge hidden problems from his pockets like loose change.

At night, Kate and Giovanna ate in local trattorias, then sat in Giovanna's huge apartment, sipping wine and talking lazily. How pleasant it must be to live like Giovanna, surrounded by beauty, by beautiful objects, so many of which had been in her family for generations. The years slid through their conversation, looping around, forming a fragile, shifting lace. "Is it possible?" Giovanna said. "We're older than your mother was when we met."

"Too strange," Kate said. "Too scary." When she dropped by every week or so now to check on her mother, Kate would often find her asleep in a chair, her head dropping sideways, her mouth slightly open. "Most of the time she's still fairly true to form, thank heavens. She's attached the one available old gent around and she's running him ragged. He simply beams. All the sweet local widows are still standing at his door, clutching their pies and pot roasts. They don't know what hit them. You know, all those years, when Baker and I were having so much trouble and neither of us quite understood what was happening and the kids were frantic and the house was pandemonium all the time—just as we'd all start screaming at each other, the phone would ring and there she'd be, saying, 'So, how is everyone enjoying this beautiful Sunday afternoon?' Now the phone rings and she says, 'Kate! What are you doing at home on a Saturday night?' "

"Ah, well." Giovanna lit a cigarette, kindling its forbidden fragrance. "She's having an adventure. And what about you?"

"Me!" Kate said. "Me?"

"What about that guy you wrote me about a year or two ago—Rover, Rower . . ."

"Rowan. Oh, lord. Blair was very enthusiastic about that one. One day she said to me, 'Mother, where's this going, this thing with Rowan?' I said, '*Going?* I'm almost fifty!' "

Giovanna exhaled a curtain of smoke. From behind it, her steady gaze rested on Kate. "You broke it off?"

"Give me a drag, please. Of course not. Though to tell you the truth, I just don't feel the need to put myself through all that again. I really don't. Anyhow, the day came, naturally, when he said he wasn't, guess what, ready for *commitment*—he actually used the word—so soon after his divorce. And then naturally the *next* day came, when I heard he'd married a twenty-three-year-old."

"You should live here." Giovanna yawned. "Here in Europe, you still have the chance to lose your lovers to someone your own age."

Much nicer, they'd agreed, clinking glasses.

There was no stone, arch, column, pediment, square inch of painting in the vicinity that Harry couldn't expound upon. He knew what pirates had lived in which of the caves below them, the Latin names of the trees, all twisted by wind, the composition of the rocks . . . Did Kate see the dome way off there? They didn't have time to stop, unfortunately, but it was a very important church, as no doubt she knew, built by X in the twelfth century, rebuilt by Y in the thirteenth, then built again on the orders of the Archbishop of Z . . . Inside there was a wonderful Annunciation by A, a wonderful pietà by B, and of course she'd seen reproductions, hadn't she, of the altarpiece . . .

It wasn't fair. He expected everyone to be as yielding to beautiful objects as he was, as easily transported. Her expression, she hoped, as the avalanche of information—art gossip—rained down, was not the one she saw daily on the faces of her students. Her poor, exasperating students, so resentful, so uncomprehending . . . The truth was that most of them had so many problems in their lives that each precious, clarifying fragment Kate struggled to hand over to them was just one more intrusion. Yet there she stood, day after day, talking, talking, talking . . . And every once in a while—she could see it—it was as if a door opened in a high stone wall.

". . . but I'm boring you," Harry was saying. "You're a serious person! And my life, I'm afraid, has been devoted, frivolously, to beauty."

True, true, she was a grunting barbarian, he was a rarified esthete. She was a high-school biology teacher, he was a—well, he was a what, exactly? As far as she could gather, whatever it was he did seemed to involve finding art or rarities, oddities, for collectors and billionaires and grotesquely expensive hotels. He'd traveled all over, there'd been a wife or two, his family had come from everywhere—Central Asia, all around the Mediterranean . . .

"Mendelssohn or salsa?" He waved a handful of CD's "To— what is it? To soothe our savage— Ack!" He honked and swerved as a giant tour bus in front of them braked shudderingly on the precipitous incline. "They have no idea how to drive! Simply not a clue!"

For miles before and behind them, caravans of tour buses clogged the road, winding along the cliffs. "Is there always this much traffic?" Kate asked.

"From now through October it will be sheer hell," Harry announced with satisfaction, as though he'd only been waiting for an opening. "And why do they come here? For what? We'll see them later, shuffling around in the churches while the guides shout and flap their arms. Blinking, loading their cameras . . . They'd much prefer to be at Disney World. They are at Disney World. Little ducks and mice frolic with them along the road of life. So why come to bother us here, on this road? Ah, we'll never know, we'll never know. And neither will they."

"Americans, I suppose," Kate said meekly.

"Not necessarily, my dear." Harry reached over and patted her hand. "Imbeciles pour in from all over."

One was supposed to get used to things, Kate thought, not find them increasingly annoying; that was the point of getting older. And how old was he, anyhow? It stood to reason that he was around her age. Probably a few years older.

Though actually, he looked no age in particular. He was wildly vigorous and agile, and an urgent, clocklike energy pulsed off him. He'd ordered wine when they'd stopped for lunch, in a restaurant overhanging the cliffs where they'd soon be driving again, and her heart had dropped along with the level of alcohol in the bottle, to the very bottom. Harry, however, showed no sign of having consumed a thing. "Don't worry," he'd said as they left—whether noting some expression she'd failed to inhibit, or engaging in a private dialogue— "I'm not drunk." And indeed, though the coastline waved back and forth beneath them like streamers and the racy little car flew out over the heart-stopping curves, it snapped back onto the road as if it were attached by elastic. Way below them, the water sparkled and ruffled, on and on and on.

It was late in the afternoon by the time they reached their destination. Majestic and serene, the hotel rose up in front of them with the terraced cliffs, the clouds, the trees, as if it had sprung from a magic seed.

Harry chivalrously swung her suitcase from the trunk and

carried it into the lobby. "What on earth do you have in here?" Rowan would have asked, smiling to illustrate that he wasn't criticizing her. Harry, of course, was completely indif-ferent. Or perhaps he knew perfectly well what weighed those hundreds of pounds—all the jars of things she'd taken, humil-iatingly, to smearing on her skin or swallowing.

And what about Harry's elegant little accoutrement, hardly bigger than a briefcase? What could he have fitted into that? A set of tiny tools, no doubt—wrenches, screwdrivers, brushes—with which to disassemble himself and clean his parts . . .

The hotel, vast as it was, had apparently been a private villa at some time. The cool sound of bells and leaf-scented air pooled here and there in the lobby. Afternoon sunlight, yellow as wildflowers, drowsed on the floors. Marble, stone, wood seemed to breathe faintly . . .

Splendid in uniform, the men at the desk opened their arms at the sight of Harry, tilting their heads to the side and exclaiming softly with delight. As they came forward, he clasped their hands, speaking a few words to each, like the true king returning. They were now referring to her, Kate re-alized at a certain point. One of the men caught her look of slight confusion and addressed her in English. "We were dis-cussing, signora, which room would be most suitable for you. It would be possible either the Rose Room, which has a fire-place and a magnificent four-poster bed. Or the room at the easternmost end of the hotel is also available, with a balcony overlooking the water."

She glanced at Harry. "It doesn't matter," he said expan-sively. "They're both lovely rooms." He turned to the desk clerk. "Perhaps the East Room—" He gave her a brief, inquir-ing smile. "—Yes. The signora might enjoy breakfasting on her balcony."

Oh, right—she'd been meant to speak, but never mind. How wonderful, just to go upstairs now, to sink back against giant feather pillows . . . A man in a red and gold jacket stood slightly behind her with her suitcase. Well, yes, of course— *Harry* wasn't going to show her to her room.

"Well—" she turned toward him and held out her hand "—you must be exhausted."

"Not at all," he said, taking her hand absently and glancing around as if for a place to put it. "I never get tired."

Just as she'd feared. And it seemed that there were several churches, several villas, a little museum, and an ex-convent that were absolutely obligatory.

"And would you care to wash up?" he said instructively. "We'll find one another in the bar." As she followed the bellman out of the lobby, she glimpsed, from the corner of her eye, Harry bending to kiss the beringed claw of an ancient lady in black, almost hidden within the wings of an enormous brocaded chair.

Kate followed, up a flowing staircase and along silent corridors. The bellman opened the massive wooden door to her room, and then the French doors onto her balcony. Lordy! No wonder no one else in the lobby looked much like a schoolteacher. Water gleams fleeted in, rocking the room gently; the high ceiling curved above her, and the stone floors floated underfoot.

Though she took as little time as possible, only slipping her few things onto the satiny hangers and splashing at her face, when she reached the bar Harry had almost emptied a glass of something. "Ah!" he said, leaping to his feet as though she'd been dawdling for an hour. "Oh. But forgive me—will you have something to drink before we set off, or would you prefer a look around before the light goes completely?"

He led her rapidly through the churches, the ex-convent, the now-public villas, bounding up and down the steep town steps and cobbled streets, providing scholarly commentary. She was *worse*, she thought, than her students—than the tourists from the buses! Who were indeed standing around town in bewildered-looking herds, uneasily gripping their cameras as though they were passports.

"Good—" Harry said, striding through the garden leading to the little museum. "—still open!" His gesture, which swept the paintings, the small mounted sculptures, was proprietary.

He was looking at a lump of stone in a glass case. No, a head; a stone coronet sat on heavy twists of stone hair over a dreaming stone face. A real girl must have modeled for it, Kate thought—an actual princess, or a young queen.

Or possibly some girl right off the streets for whom the artist had conceived a passion. Had she lived to be old? It was hard to imagine this girl old. Trouble, she looked like; pure trouble. A provocative reserve emanated from the faint stone smile, sending a hiss of fire through the stone-cooled air. Trouble even now, Kate thought. This girl had seen to it that the sculptor's obsession would be inflicted on whoever saw her for all time to come.

Kate glanced at Harry for a translation of the bit of text on the glass case, but he had turned away, to an elaborate marble, whose racing lines were taking a moment to resolve in front of her. A faun, or possibly a satyr, something with furry haunches and little hooves and horns had seized a young woman from behind. Her head was arched way back against him and her long hair whipped around her face, which was slightly contorted. Her eyes were almost closed. One of the creature's hands was splayed out between the girl's sharp pelvic bones, and the other pinned her own hand to one of her adolescent breasts. Her free arm reached out, with what intent it was impossible to guess—it had broken off at the elbow. Kate stumbled slightly on an uneven stone underfoot. "Goodness me," she said.

"Yes, marvelous—" Harry glanced at his watch. "Second century after Christ, probably a copy of a Greek piece. Are we through here? The church I particularly want you to see closes in minutes."

In the lobby, the delicate afternoon had given way to a rich, deep twinkling. More people had arrived; the bellboys, in their red and gold, were loading huge leather cases onto trolleys. The tapping of high heels echoed faintly from the corridors. "Dinner at eight-thirty?" Harry said. "By the way, how did you find your room—satisfactory?"

"Glorious," Kate said. "It's . . . *glorious* . . ."

"Glorious." He smiled at her and briefly her arms and legs seemed to need rearrangement; what did one generally do with them? "Well, very good then. We'll have a bit of a rest, yes? And meet in the bar."

Dinner at eight-thirty. Once again, they'd be sitting at a table together. But what had she imagined was going to happen? They could hardly have dinner separately.

She found her room waiting; the crisp linen had been turned down, mysteriously, the heavy shutters drawn. She was being attended to, as if she—of all people, she thought—had come upon the palace where the poor Beast waited for his release. She sat for a while on the balcony, watching ribbons of mist twine below her through the trees and listening to distant bells from hidden fields and towns. Grass, petal, wave, stone turned to velvet—indistinct glowing patches—as veil on veil of twilight dropped over them.

A jar of aromatic bath salts had been provided. She poured

them like a libation under the faucet—why not? They represented her salary—and took a long soak, moving from time to time to solicit the water's musical response.

One assumed there was such a thing as chance; when one was young, one assumed that the way one's life was to express itself was one of many possible ways, and later, one assumed that this had been true.

Of course, even if she hadn't married Baker, she'd never have been living like this. She'd never have been living like Giovanna, casually surrounded by silk-covered furniture and lovely, old pieces of glass and silver, entertaining herself in her spare time with one admirer or another. Those things were probably not within the compass of her particular possibilities.

But surely it was within that compass—surely, with one degree's alteration here or there—that she and Baker would not have married. And if they had not, if they hadn't had children, one thing was certain—that Baker would now mean no more to her than any young man she might have met in the course of her school duties; she'd have a harmless memory of a nice young man.

And from all the years with him? You couldn't feel love once it was gone. What you could feel for a long time was the sorrow of its fading, like the burning afterimage of a setting sun. And then that was gone, too. What she would remember for the rest of her life was the fact, at least, of the shocking pain they'd been forced to inflict on one another. Eventually when they'd touched, it was like touching a wound.

When both the children had left for school, she'd expected a long period of lonely freedom, an expansion. But now that Baker was sick, Blair and Brice hovered closely, as if it were she who needed consolation, not they. Blair asked questions continuously. *Why did you and Dad . . . How did you feel when . . .*

They'd been over and over it all from the children's adolescence on. "I've told you what I can," Kate said. "I'm sorry. It was moving very fast back then."

But at the time it hadn't felt fast. There were long days of paralysis, sleepless nights. How could so much anguish have been expended on something that now seemed so remote?

"What can I say to you?" she told Blair. "I had a reasonably civil relationship with my parents, but I never understood them. I don't suppose their life together was entirely without chaos and misery, but I have no idea what went on between them. Or within either of them, actually. Of course you don't understand us. No one has ever understood their parents. And what, for that matter, do I know about you?"

Blair stared at Kate, tears spilling up into her eyes. "You knew it was me from the *back* that time, going by in Jeffrey's car at about eighty, even though I was supposedly at *Jennifer's*!"

Kate sighed. "That's different," she'd said.

She wrapped herself in a vast, soft towel and contemplated her clothing. A faint breeze came through the French doors and the black dress swayed slightly on its hanger.

It was a dress that she'd recklessly allowed Blair to talk her into buying from a terrifying shop in Chicago. That evening she'd thought of its cost and actually covered her face in embarrassment—of course she'd return it. But then, the sight of it swathed in its tissue paper . . .

It was a little daring, that dress. Nonetheless, she'd gone out in it several times, before Rowan came to his senses and married an infant.

She reached over to the hanger. It was now or never. She slipped the dress over her head and breathed in; the zipper climbed, cinching her tightly. She turned to challenge the mirror: now or never.

All right, then—never, the mirror said, coolly. And what did she think this was—a *date*?

The bar was almost filled. The tender glimmer from candles and lamps embraced the encampments of guests; bright little clusters of laughter bloomed here and there amid clinking glass and conversation. Harry was sitting at the far end of the room, his back to her.

Kate's hands went cold. He was with people. A family, it seemed. A pretty girl, just a little older, Kate judged, than her students, was stretched out on a recamier, in a display of intense boredom. The father was a great, blocky affair, wearing a blazer with gold buttons, and a little boy in an identical blazer perched stiffly on a settee.

The woman next to the boy leaned toward Harry, her red-nailed fingers playing with a large solitaire at her throat. "Really!" Kate heard her exclaim, and she laughed gaily. Her toenails were the fevered red of her fingernails and her lipstick. Her little white suit was as tense as an origami construction, but a snippet of lace peeked out aggressively from under the jacket.

Harry was gesticulating; his voice came into focus: ". . . insisted, but *insisted*—" he was saying, "—that I jump on the Concorde. What could I do? A call from Dubzhinski. In New York I literally scampered to make my connection. I fell off the plane in Los Angeles, and was at the Polo Lounge in seconds. I took her out of my case, unwrapped her, and set her down in front of us on the bar. There she was, with her little chin thrust forward and her hands clasped behind her back, and those astonishing legs. Dubzhinski was trembling. I could actually hear that tiny, hard heart of his. It was hammering away like a cash register at Christmastime. He was paralyzed, he stared, and then he reached out and upended her to look under her tutu. 'Go ahead,' I said, 'we can authenticate her right here.' And the next—"

The wife was glancing sidelong at Kate with slight alarm, as though Kate might be hoping to sell them pencils. Harry swiveled in his chair, looked at her blankly, then sprang to his feet. "My dear!" he said. "Ah, we're a chair short! What shall, what shall, what shall we do, eh?"

For a moment everyone except the girl was standing and bobbing about and pushing one another toward seats. "Oh," Kate began. "Well, I could just—" Just what? But then a murmuring waiter in a white coat was there with a smile of compassion for her that pierced her like a bayonet.

Harry and the Reitzes had met several years before, in Paris, it was explained, at the home of a mutual friend, about whom they'd just been reminiscing.

"Oh, Franz and I couldn't really claim that M. Dubzhinski is a *friend*. We just happened to be with the LaRues. But you know—" Mrs. Reitz addressed Kate "—that house is even more gorgeous than in the pictures." She turned back to Harry, but her perfume continued to loiter thuggishly around Kate. "I know there are people who say M. Dubzhinski is . . . Well. But he was charming to me that time. Simply charming."

" 'Charming . . .' " Mr. Reitz tried out the word and smiled pityingly. "I wouldn't entirely agree. But harmless enough at bottom. Colorful, as the expression goes. I believe it was one of your countrymen—" he nodded at Kate "—who put it so well: *I've never met a man I didn't like.*"

The girl sat up slowly, fluffing her long hair back. "Really?" she glanced at him. "I have."

Mrs. Reitz's eyes were not quite closed. Her face was

more unresponsive than if she hadn't heard at all. But Mr. Reitz was speaking to Kate. "My wife, too, is American."

Was the girl's arrogance affected, or was it entirely real? As cocky as Kate's students could be, as irritating, they were actually, for all their show, quite humble. Of course, Kate had never encountered a child as privileged as this girl, with this hard candy gloss . . . "Texas," Mrs. Reitz was saying, leaning over to touch Kate's wrist, her own flashing and clanging with jewelry. "But I guess you heard that, right off! I wouldn't change Zurich for anything, but I get homesick. I miss Los Angeles. I miss Dallas. I miss New York."

"I'm from Cincinnati," Kate said.

"Oh." Mrs. Reitz's smile was puzzled. "I see."

"I'm really just visiting," Kate said.

"Ah," Mrs. Reitz said archly.

"No," Kate said. "A friend in Rome."

"A mutual friend," Harry said fussily, as he snagged a waiter. "Champagne? Champagne, my dear?" he asked Kate and then the girl, who had been drinking nothing. "Good. And another round for the rest of us, thank you. Yes, this kind lady has been good enough to accompany me thus far and have a little look at the area. Tomorrow she returns, I believe, do you not?"

"How nice," Mrs. Reitz said. Her gaze swept Kate's flowered dress, her face, her cardigan, and lapsed from Kate like a cat's.

"We're going up to Rome ourselves tomorrow or Sunday," Mr. Reitz said.

"We're doing the palaces on the kids' spring break," Mrs. Reitz explained.

"The question is," Mr. Reitz said, "which day exactly will we travel? We're told that the traffic is quite terrible on Saturday. But also we're told that the traffic is quite terrible on Sunday."

"That is true," Harry said. He looked at one child, then the other. "Are you glad to be on holiday?"

The boy nodded vigorously. "Yes, thank you."

"And you?" Harry asked.

The girl, who was reclining again, opened her eyes and looked steadily at him. "Not madly." She closed her eyes again and crossed her arms over her chest, as though she were sunbathing, or dying.

"Sit up, sweetheart," Mrs. Reitz murmured. "Well!" she said, casting a misty look at the room in general. "At least we've been lucky with the weather. They said it's been raining and raining and raining," she explained to Kate. "I was afraid it was going to rain today."

"But it didn't," Mr. Reitz said.

"No," Mrs. Reitz agreed. "It didn't."

"We have good luck with the weather," Mr. Reitz said, "but bad luck with the traffic. It took us all day to get here. We expected to arrive at three o'clock. But we arrived almost at seven."

The girl emitted a small sigh, which floated down among them like a feather.

"Now, *you've* determined it's best to drive up tomorrow . . ." Mrs. Reitz furrowed deferentially at Kate, as though Kate were a senior scholar of traffic.

"I'll be taking the train," Kate said.

"The train!" Mrs. Reitz said. "What a *marvelous*—"

"I want to take the train," the little boy said mournfully. "I wanted to take the train," he explained to Kate. "But we can't because of the Porsche."

"That's the problem, sweetie," Mrs. Reitz said absently,

reaching over to a small silver bowl of mixed nuts, which Harry was nervously plundering. "Excuse me!" he said, retracting his hand as though it had been bitten.

"I am so sorry!" Mrs. Reitz exclaimed. "Oh, I am simply starving."

"I can imagine," Harry said distractedly.

"And I suppose spring holidays are the reason for all this damned, if you'll pardon me, traffic," Mr. Reitz said. "Yes, the only occasions on which one has the opportunity to travel with one's family, others are traveling with theirs. What a paradox!"

The boy's straw slurped among the ice at the bottom of his drink.

"Darling," Mrs. Reitz said. "Your father was merely making an observation."

The boy blushed red. "My baby," Mrs. Reitz said. She drew him to her and stroked his silky hair, smiling first at her husband, then at Harry. "You know, I absolutely adore this place. It's so romantic. Don't you just keep imagining all the things that must have gone on in these rooms? Oh, my. For hundreds of years!" The boy sat stock still until his mother released him, recrossing her legs and primly readjusting the hem of her little skirt.

"Good heavens—" Harry glanced at his watch "—they'll have been waiting with our table! I do wish we could ask you to join us, but, that is, they're very strict. Please excuse us."

"What an ordeal!" he said to Kate as they were seated. "How horrible! Was I terribly rude? I suppose I should have invited them to dine with us. And why not? Would it be possible for them to bore us any more than they already have? But yes, on reflection, yes. I feel I might still recover."

The dining room was an aerie, a bower, hung with a playful lattice of garlands. Its white tile floors were adorned with painted baskets of fruit, and there were real ones scattered here and there on stands. But even as the waiters glided by with trays of glossy roasted vegetables and platters of fish, even while Harry took it upon himself to order for her, knowledgeably and solicitously, Kate felt tainted. Despite the room's conceit that eating was a pastime for elves and fairies, Mrs. Reitz's carnality had disclosed the truth: this aggregation of hairy vertebrates, scrubbed, scented, prancing about on hind legs, was ruthlessly bent on physical gratifications—tactile, visual, gustatory, genital . . . The candles! The flowers! A trough providing mass feedings for naked guests would be less pornographic.

The Reitzes were being led to their own table. Mrs. Reitz waggled one set of fingers in their direction, holding her jacket closed beneath her collarbones with the other, as if an enormous wind were about to whip it open, exposing her.

"One encounters these terrible people wherever one goes," Harry said. "They all know me—it's the unfortunate side of my work, if I can use such an elevated term for, actually, my little hobby . . . They're all clients, or friends of clients. Clients of clients . . ."

Despite Mrs. Reitz's speedy (and uncalled for!) assessment of Kate as out of the running, Kate thought, Mrs. Reitz was probably not much younger, really. The bouncing gold hair, the vivacity, the strained skin suggested it . . .

All those years ago, when she'd finally confessed to her mother about Baker and Norman, Kate had waited quietly through her mother's initial monologue. "Don't worry," her mother said grimly. "I won't say I told you so."

In fact, she never had told Kate so. On the contrary, she'd been elated by Baker's family, his appearance, his education, his law firm . . . "I can't say I'm overly surprised about . . . this other person, but does he have to move *out*? Why can't people of your generation set aside your personal appetites for one instant? The children are going to be confused enough as it is! Oh, I simply can't believe he's leaving you for— for— for *an electrician*! Well, but I'm sure he'll continue to support you."

Kate had smiled faintly. "You are? He's going into public-interest law."

"My God, my God!" her mother cried. "Oh, I suppose I should feel compassion for him. He was always so weak, so lost. But why did he have to marry you? Why did he feel he had the right to ruin your life while he was working things out for himself? Well, and yet I can understand it. I suppose he thought you could help him. You were always such a sweet girl. And not, if you don't mind my saying so, very threatening, sexually."

"And the worst thing," Harry was saying, "is that they all seem to want something from me. I don't know what! Perhaps they imagine I'll be able to pick up some piece for a song, something to transform a salon from the ordinarily to the spectacularly vulgar. Some great, blowsy, romping nymph with an enormous behind . . ."

Kate contemplated him as he talked decoratively on. One had to acknowledge, even admire, such energy, so strong a will to enjoy, to entertain, even if, as was clearly the case, it was only to entertain himself.

"Giovanna tells me you're a teacher," he said unexpectedly, laying down his fork and knife as if her response required his full attention.

"Nothing very exalted, I'm afraid," Kate said. "Just high school biology."

"It sounds rather exalted to me," he said. "I should think it would be rather a beautiful subject."

Kate glanced at him. "It is, actually. Hmmm . . ." She noted

the sudden haloed clarity of her thought, the detailed vibrancy of her awareness, and concluded she was drunk. Natural enough—she'd certainly been drinking. "I have to admit
that I do find it beautiful. Of course, what I teach is very rudimentary—basic evolutionary theory, simple genetic princi-
ples, taxonomies, a lot of structural stuff. Pretty much what I
learned myself in school. You know, an oak tree, a tadpole, the
shape of its growth, the way the organism works . . ."

"I understand nothing about biology," he said. "Nothing,
nothing, nothing at all . . ."

"Oh, well. Neither do I, really." Kate found she was laughing loudly. She composed herself. "I mean, not what's going
on now, all the fantastic molecular frontiers, the borders with
chemistry, physics . . . the real mysteries . . ."

He rested his chin on the backs of his clasped hands
and gazed at her. "What seems so simple to you—a tree, a
tadpole—those things are completely mysterious to me!"

"Actually, I'm not being at all—" Was he, in fact, interested? Well, it wasn't her place to judge. At least he was pre-
tending to be. At least he was— Stop that, she told herself; a
conversation was something that humans had. "I mean, I'm
not being . . . Because actually it's all hugely . . . It brings you
to your knees, really, doesn't it? You know, it's really quite
funny—there are my students, rows of little humans, staring at
me. And there I am, a human, staring right back. And I'm
holding up pictures! Charts! Of what's inside us. And the students write things down in their notebooks. Our hearts are
pumping, the blood is going round and round, our lungs are
bringing air in and out . . . *Class, look at the pictures. These are our
lungs, our kidneys, our stomachs, our veins and arteries, our spleens,
our brains, our hearts* . . . There we are, looking at *pictures* of
what's going on every instant inside our very own bodies!"

"I don't even yet have it straight. Where any of those things are," Harry said ruefully. "My kidneys, my spleen, my heart . . ."

Kate shook her head. "It's a wonder we can understand anything at all about ourselves . . . We can't even see our own kidneys."

"Ah!" Harry grunted. "So I have recovered, after all." He summoned the waiter to order for Kate a little chalice of raspberries and scented froth, then sat back to observe as she took the first spoonful. "Extraordinary, no?" he said. "It's up to you. I'm not allowed." He smiled briefly and shallowly, then rubbed his forehead. "To tell you the truth, it's a rather stressful trip for me, always—going back to this little farmhouse of mine. I spent summers there in my childhood . . . Really, I'm very glad to have had a pretext for stopping here overnight."

Harsh tears shot up to Kate's eyes. Fatigue, she thought. "Tell me . . ."

"Yes?"

"Tell me . . . Oh—well, tell me, then . . . Have you known Giovanna long?"

"For many centuries. Our families are vaguely intertwined, though I never met her until I was a young man. There was a party, very grand, and in all the enormous crowd, women in spectacular gowns, I caught a glimpse of a young girl. I remember every detail of that glimpse—the exact posture, the smile, every button on the dress. She was scarcely thirteen. There were eight years between us."

His hand was resting on the table, three, maybe four inches from hers. "There were?" The cuff of his shirt was very white. She raised her eyes from it to smile at him. "Aren't there still?"

He sat back and studied her, amusement and sorrow competing in his own smile. "Well, now it's a different eight years." He sighed, and signaled for the check.

"Oh, please, let me. You did lunch, and drinks. You've taken all this time—"

"Madam," he said gently. "You will put your purse away for this one evening, please. But will you join me for a last drink in the bar? A digestif. And I will have, if you won't find it too disgusting, a cigar."

But the Reitzes were already ensconced again in the bar, and waved them over. Kate glanced at Harry, but he had gone completely unreadable; he had simply disappeared.

Mrs. Reitz slid to one side of her settee and patted the space next to her. Again, there was a scuffle. Harry won, and Kate found herself sitting with Mrs. Reitz, suffocating under a dome of her perfume like a dying bug, while he went off to commandeer a chair.

Well. All right. Fine. And a very good thing it was, actually, that Norman was an electrician! He'd completely rewired her little house. And that at a time when she was barely getting by, even with the money Baker managed to scrape up for the kids.

The waiter was already prepared with a cigar for Harry, undoubtedly in accord with ancient custom. "Here, please," Mr. Reitz said. "One of those for me, too."

"Oh, dear—" Mrs. Reitz fluttered toward Kate. "I know men have to have them, but I never get used to them, do you?"

"I never get used to anything—" Kate was startled by her own slightly swaggering tone. "I mean, except for the things that aren't happening any longer."

"That's an interesting way of putting it . . ." Mrs. Reitz said cautiously.

Good. Kate had frightened her. But heavens! What was her—Why was she so— After all, Harry had stated quite clearly that he was repentant about having snubbed these people before dinner. The girl was slung out sullenly upon a curvy white and gold chair, far above the juvenile sniping of her elders.

"Ooch," Mr. Reitz said, patting the prairielike region of his stomach. "It's impossible to speak after such a meal. But, really, have you no good advice for us? Saturday, or Sunday, to Rome."

"Whichever you choose—" Harry exhaled with pleasure "—you will wish you had chosen the other."

"Let us be prudent," Mr. Reitz said. "We will play the early bird. Let us be ready to make our final decision at breakfast. *If*—" he turned to the girl "—we think we can get up in good time, for a change."

The girl lifted a long, shining hair from her dress and considered it. "We'll do our best," she said.

"I surely do envy you," Mrs. Reitz said. "This little girl of mine has a talent for sleep. But I can never sleep near the sea at all. It makes me so *rest*less . . ."

"The sea?" Mr. Reitz said. "Restless? How very original. One is always learning the most surprising new things about one's spouse! But it's a good thing then about our room. I must say, I was quite annoyed earlier with the staff. I had my secretary specifically request the view. They swore she never did, but a people which is known for its charm is not often known also for its honesty."

"I have a terrible time sleeping in hotels, myself," Harry said. "Unfortunately, I'm always in hotels these days . . . How did it happen, how did it happen? Oh, it's hard to believe, isn't it, that it's the same person who has lived each bit of one's life.

Yes, an hour or two of sleep, and then I'm up again, wandering around all night. In fact, I'd best go up now and try to get some sleep before I lose my chance."

Kate attempted to smile pleasantly. "I think I'll go up now, too."

"And how is your room, my dear?" Harry asked.

Kate looked at him. Why hadn't she just gone directly up after dinner?

"Good heavens, yes, where is my brain!" he said. "Glorious. Of course, you said—glorious."

He did in fact lie in his room for an hour or so, letting images of the girl play over his nerves. Her exquisite throat, the curve of her cheek . . . the clear, poreless skin, so close in color to the brows, the lashes, the light, long hair . . . her startling greenish blue eyes. She was clever about clothes, obviously—that mother surely hadn't chosen the dress, simple, and stylishly long, stopping just at narrow shins. On her feet she wore elegant straw sandals.

When the buzzing of the girl in his head grew unbearable, he would convert it into thoughts of the astonishing Russian sleigh bed he had come across in an antique store that he would pass by again on his way to the farmhouse tomorrow. Things, things—at his age! But it seemed that age only increased his appetite to acquire.

The shop was one of several in the area he returned to often, ostensibly to pick up an item for one client or another. These places sometimes came into possession of surprisingly good pieces—occasionally an object that perhaps would have been consigned to a museum had it not, fortunately, fallen into ignorant hands, to be rescued then by him.

He had bought the most fetching little Madonna at one of them on his last trip. He noted the bed at the time, but the Madonna had simply absorbed all his attention, until he got her settled into the right spot. Only then did he begin to remember the bed—its fluent maple curves, its allusion to careless pleasure . . . This time he would buy it for certain. Assuming it was still there! Oh, why hadn't he called weeks ago, when he realized how badly he wanted it?

But the problem remained: Where to put it—Rome? Paris? Both places were small, and he already had remarkable beds in each . . .

He could move one of them out here, to the farmhouse. But that was the point. He always meant to be emptying the place out so he could sell it. And yet, each time he saw it. . . Those summers, when he was ten, eleven, twelve . . . Those were happy years, insofar as years could be said to be happy. Years filled with sensations so potent they seemed like clues to a riddle.

The place wouldn't bring much of anything, once the money was divided between himself and his surviving brother. It was a nuisance; it would simply eat cash if it were to be kept from falling to bits. His brother, and his own sons, one in Istanbul, one in London, showed no particular interest in it. Only he, only he was enslaved by the memory of the sun on the leaves around the door, the way the fruit tasted in the morning . . .

It was dark when you entered. As you opened the shutters, grand, churchly prisms turned everything in their path to phantoms. The cool aroma of the waxed stone floors blended with the smell of sun-warmed herbs. First the big room, then the room they'd used informally as a library, then the huge kitchen . . . At the long wooden table, almost transparent in the light falling from the high window, sat the girl. Water dripped slowly somewhere, onto crockery or stone. He turned, readjusting his pillow. Perhaps he had slept for some minutes.

The bar was now empty except for a sprawling group of five or six men and a woman, which was scaling peaks of drunken happiness—a TV crew, the waiter told him; they had filmed a commercial nearby that day. One of them was pounding away on a small piano in a corner, and the others sang along, loudly and terribly, arms around shoulders. Harry sipped a cognac and regarded them with melancholy affection. They were still young, almost young. For an instant he could see, as if it were incandescently mapped, the path of years that lay ahead of each of them, its particular sorrows, joys, terrors . . . He'd have one drink, and return to his room.

When the girl appeared in the doorway, he restrained himself from jumping to his feet. For a moment he hadn't understood that she was real.

She approached; he stood and bent over her hand.

"I thought I might find Mother down here," she said vaguely.

Wordlessly, he pulled out a chair for her.

"Huh. Well, I guess Franz has learned to sleep with his eyes open," she said. "May I have a drink, please?"

He was glad for the excuse to walk over to the bar and stand there for some moments while glasses were warmed and cognacs were poured; his brains were in such a clamor that he'd hardly been able to hear what she had said, let alone make sense of it. The TV crew was now singing an American popular song, stumbling over the words and filling in with la-

la–las. Harry had read somewhere recently about the woman who'd written the song and recorded it. She'd grown up in a ghetto, he recalled, impoverished; the song was the story of her life.

The girl stared down at the little candle on the table, in an aureole of her own silence, impervious to the racket of the TV crew. After a few minutes he dared to speak. "Do you go to school in Zurich?"

She lifted an eyebrow. "Fortunately not. I'm at a boarding school in the States. One more year, and I'm free."

Tears kept coming to his eyes, as if he had been broken open; impressions, almost visible, were floating up around him, released from the hidden world by an enchanted touch: damp leaves and earth, a dappled meadow—treasure no doubt collected by his yielding and ravenous childhood senses, and stored. Every once in a while, some magic girl could unlock it. Then how to keep aloft in the radiant ether?

"Actually, I've hardly lived in Zurich at all," she said. "Mother married Franz when I was eleven, and they shipped me off to school when I was thirteen. I spent summers with my father, anyhow."

"And where does he live, my dear?"

"Oh, he's still near Dallas. Bossing a bunch of cows around. He's got some new kids . . ." She propped herself up at the table on her elbows, her long, delicate forearms together, her chin in her palms. "Mother and Franz! What a joke."

He smiled gently. "It's quite mysterious, what attracts one human being to another . . ."

"Not in this case," she said. "I mean, did you notice the size of his bank account?" She frowned, studying the small flame in front of her. "So . . . Mother said you have places all over."

"Really," he said. "All over?"

"But— I mean, where do you live?"

"Here and there. Like you."

Her green-blue gaze lingered on him, then withdrew. "She said you've got a title, too."

"Oh, lying around in a drawer somewhere."

She poked at the soft wax of the candle for a few moments, allowing him to watch her. "So, why don't you use it?" she asked.

"Evidently it's not necessary!"

She glanced at him quizzically, then smiled to herself and poked again at the candle. "Okay . . . Well, your turn . . ."

"My turn . . . All right . . . Well, why off to school at such a tender age?"

"Want to guess? Or want me to tell you."

He was sorry he'd raised the question. Any number of scenarios, all of them sordid, sprang to mind.

"I bet you can guess."

"No," he said. "You needn't—"

"Because Mother thought I was having an affair. With my piano teacher."

How many more years was his heart going to stand the sort of strain to which he was subjecting it now? "And were you?" he asked, against his will.

"Not exactly. You know. I'd go over to his apartment after school with my schoolbooks and my sheet music and my little uniform. Mother loved it that I had to wear a uniform, obviously. She'd still have me in anklets and hair ribbons if she could. And one day Mr. Schulte sort of wrestled me off the piano bench onto the floor. I mean, he left my uniform on. I guess he liked it, too. And then we'd work on Brahams. So that's sort of how it went every Tuesday. He hardly ever spoke to me, except for, you know, you should practice more, watch the tempo here, don't hold your wrists like that, this is legato . . ." She glanced at Harry speculatively, then sat back demurely with her drink.

How pitiable she was. Her bravado, her coarseness, her self-involvement—completely innocent. Perhaps never again would she be so dazzled by the primacy of her own life. "Was he—"

"The first, uh-huh. Not Franz, if that's what you were thinking. No slummy boys in an alley . . ."

It was not what he'd intended to ask. No matter. He closed his eyes and listened to her clear voice; behind the shining veil, she continued to talk.

". . . The sad fact is that Mother had this humongous crush on Schulte, it was totally obvious. He was always sort of kissing her hand and, you know, *gazing* at her with big, soulful eyes . . ." The girl sighed langorously. "Actually, I have to admit he was kind of attractive, in a creepy kind of way . . ."

One of the singers had toppled off her heights of drunken joy and was now crying; a few of the others were embracing her, mussing her hair, singing into her ear, and attempting to rock her to the music, such as it was. The girl directed an abstracted stare of distaste in their direction, then looked away, obliterating them. The word "kidney," throbbing on a flat, stylized shape, hung for an instant in Harry's mind. Then the girl dangled her empty glass by the stem and Harry caught his breath, seeing her in her flouncy bedroom, dangling a pen, with which she was about to record her most intimate feelings. A gilt-edged diary, a heart-shaped lock . . .

"Are you happy enough, my dear?" The question leapt urgently from him.

"Enough for what? Oh, well. It lies ahead, right?"

"It does," he said passionately, tears coming again to his eyes. "It does . . ."

An expression of pure derision passed quickly across her face.

"Ahead or behind," he amended, and the candle between them received a tiny smile. "Ahead or behind. That you can count on . . ."

Just beyond the cordial room, the world was whispering. Harry—it had been a long time since he had thought of himself as anything other than Harry, though what offhand joke or misunderstanding had landed him with the name he no longer quite remembered—closed his eyes to let the shimmering air, the faint ruffling of the sea from outside the open windows reach him, embrace him. "It's a remarkable night," he said. "Shall we walk for just a bit?"

She sighed and sat herself up in her chair, throwing her hair back over her shoulders again.

No, he must send his afflicted princess up to sleep. He would lie down, himself, drifting along on whatever currents her inebriating presence had conjured up.

"I don't know," she said, dreamily. "I was thinking. We could go upstairs. Don't you think? I mean, you could authenticate me . . ."

It seemed to him that she blushed faintly, though more likely it was only the flames that had roared up in front of his eyes. "I guess my room would be better," she continued. "When and if Franz ever starts to snore, Mother is sure to be out prowling for you."

They had put her in what they called the Rose Room, though except for the faint pinkish tone of the walls and the splendid four-poster, it was deliciously austere.

He perched on the chaise, in the muted light of the small

lamp next to it, his lovely, dark farmhouse floating near him, the night just beyond the room's closed shutters . . . Perhaps the nervous American schoolteacher was sitting on her balcony like a sentinel at the prow of a ship keeping them from harm . . . How many wonders there used to be for him! The miraculous human landscapes! Long, brilliant nights . . . Was there never to be one of those again? Whatever role he'd been assigned in the girl's drama—her drama of triumph, her drama of degradation—it was certain to be a despicable or ridiculous one. There was no chance—at least almost no chance—that she would receive from him what he so longed to provide: even a tiny portion of pleasure or solace. And when she remembered him, no doubt she would remember him with contempt.

Briefly he closed his eyes, luxuriating in the purity of her face and body, the glowing skein of sensation she was causing the air to spin out around him, his sharp thrill of longing—everything, in short, he was waiting (like a bride!) to lose. Lazily, as though moving into a trance, she dropped one piece of clothing, then another, on the floor.

When Kate awoke, it was already late. She opened her shutters and brightness was everywhere.

The night before, she'd sat for a long while on her balcony. The sky was extraordinary—terrifying, really, with great, flaring starbursts. How long had all those blades of cold light traveled in order to cross here and pass on through this one night's heart? she wondered. Trillions and trillions of years.

She would have liked to be able to return to the cozy bar for the comfort of voices around her and a glass of something soothing. But for all she knew, the Reitzes were still there.

And the fact is, women of her age were conspicuous on their own. People tended to pity, even fear you. In any case, she was hardly the sort of person who could sit alone in such a room at this hour; one more drink could be a disaster. Oh, and worst of all—the kindness of the waiters!

So she listened to the sea altering the rocks below her, the wind around her shaping the trees, as the starlight shot past. Time itself made no sound at all.

Baker had told her about Norman—he was desperately sorry, he said, his beautiful, dark eyes imploring her not to turn away; but there was nothing to be done. And there she was at the edge of a cliff. She'd been walking along, and just where she was about to take her next step, in that instant there was nothing.

So she went back to school to get a teaching degree, and then there was far too much to do to brood about Baker. Only sometimes at night she'd awaken as if falling from a ledge, crying out—landing hard against what her life had turned out to be, her bedclothes limp with sweat and tears.

After Baker had been living with Norman for a while, it was as if he'd always lived with Norman. There was only a residue of feeling when she and Baker met, exchanging the children or going about their separate lives—a sort of cold ash that faintly recorded their footsteps.

She had been luckier than a lot of her friends, as she learned bit by bit; Norman was wonderful with the children—so forthcoming, so understanding . . . and often when he came by to drop them off he'd sit in the kitchen with her, chatting over a leisurely beer. Through the years, in fact, they'd become truly close.

Terrible, the body's yearning, terrible. But you could always outwait it. First, there had been nothing in front of her,

then—however ineptly—she, the children, Baker, and Norman wove together a swaying bridge, crossing step by cautious
step over the awful chasm. And here, on the other side, Baker
was dying.

The morning lobby was bright and busy. Harry was waiting
to say goodbye to her, evidently, and the Reitzes were there,
too. Harry put down the newspaper he seemed to have been
trying to read, and stood to greet her, his arms open. "My
dear! We've only just finished breakfast. We kept hoping you'd
deign to join us."

"Yes, I slept and slept," she said.

"The sleep of the just!" Mr. Reitz said. "Like me!"

"And will we meet again?" Harry said to Kate. "Ah, who
can say, who can say . . ."

In the bright light Mrs. Reitz's skin looked dry and fragile, as she lingered near Harry. "Now, promise me," she was
saying to him, "the next time you're in Zurich—"

"Can we go now?" The girl, who had been standing at the
door watching the cars pull up and depart, turned. "I'm sorry,"
she said to Kate, "but they always say I'm holding them up.
And I've been waiting for hours!"

Kate smiled at the childish intensity of the girl's distress,
and just caught herself before smoothing back the girl's hair as
she used to Blair's when Blair would get herself into a state
over some passing trifle. "Be patient," she used to say. "Be patient. It will be over soon, it will be better tomorrow, next
week you won't even remember . . ."

WINDOW

Noah is settled down on his little blanket, and Alma has given him some spoons to play with. High up, a few feet away, Alma and Kristina drink coffee at the kitchen table. Noah, thank heavens, has been subdued since Alma opened the door to them, no trouble at all.

In this new place he seems peculiarly vivid—not entirely familiar, as if the way Alma sees him were trickling into Kristina's vision. Kristina contemplates his look of gentle inquiry, his delicate eyebrows, gold against his darker skin, his springy little ringlets. He looks distantly monumental in his beauty, like an idol at the center of a serene pond, sending out quiet ripples.

"You better do something about that cold of his. He looks like he's got a little fever," Alma says, exhaling smoke carefully away from him. "Or is that asthma?"

Kristina's gaze transfers to Alma's face.

"Does he have asthma?" Alma says.

"He'll be better now we're out of the car," Kristina says.

Yesterday afternoon and last night, and most of today, too, nothing but driving in rain, pulling over for patchy sleep, Noah waking again and again, crying, as he does these days coming out of naps, bad dreams sticking to him. Or maybe he's torn from good ones.

Or maybe dreams are new to him in general and it's frightening—one life sinking into the shadows, the forgotten one rising up. How would she know? He's talking pretty well now—he's got new words every day—but he doesn't quite have the idea yet of conversation and its uses.

Driving up, Kristina saw water just out back of the house, and tangled brush still bare of leaves, but Alma has taped plastic over her kitchen window to keep out the cold, and the plastic is blurry, and denting in the wind. All that's visible are vague, dark blotches, spreading, twisting, and disappearing. Anyone could be walking along the shore out in the gathering dark, looking in, and you wouldn't know.

Alma's saying that her friend Gerry is going to come by and then they're going out to grab a bite. "I won't be back too late, I guess." She glances at Kristina as impersonally as if she were checking something on a chart. "I'll pick up something at work tomorrow for the baby's cough." A psychiatric facility is what she called the place she works, but it sounds like a hospital.

A clattering over by the fridge makes Kristina's heart bounce, and there's a large man—stopping short in the doorway.

"Gerry, my sister Kristina," Alma says. "Kristina, Gerry."

"Your sister?" is what the man finds to say.

Alma reddens fast to an unpleasant color and looks down at her coffee cup. "Close enough. The guy who was my dad? Seems he was her dad, too."

"Hey," Gerry says, and gives Alma a little pat. But it's too late. Kristina was always the pretty one.

Gerry has a full, frowzy beard and a sheepish, tentative manner, as if it's his lot to knock over liquids or splinter chairs when he sits. Kristina picks up Noah to get him out from underfoot. "Can you say hi?" she asks him.

He observes Gerry soberly while Gerry waves, then burrows his head against her shoulder.

"Cute," Gerry says to Kristina. "Yours?"

Alma sighs. "No, ours." And then it's Gerry's turn to become red.

"Is there a store near here where I can get some milk and things for him?" Kristina asks. "We kind of ran out on the way."

Alma grinds her cigarette out on her saucer, staring at it levelly. "I would have stocked up if I'd known you were coming," she says.

"I tried to call from the road," Kristina says.

"McClure's will still be open," Gerry says.

Alma looks at him without altering her expression, and turns back to Kristina. "Gas station type place a few miles down. Not the answer to your dreams, maybe, but you'll find the essentials."

"Which way do I go?" Kristina asks.

Alma looks at her for a long moment. "If the car goes glub glub? Try turning around."

By the time Kristina returns from McClure's, Alma and Gerry are gone. Entering the house for a second time, this time with a key, juggling Noah and a bag of supplies, Kristina could practically be coming home. The mailbox says she is; that's her name there—a durable memento from the man who slid out of Alma's life soon after Alma was born and about a decade later, when Kristina was born, slid out of hers.

When Kristina first saw the house this afternoon, she had felt the sort of shame that accompanies making an error. She hadn't realized she'd been expecting anything specific, but clearly there'd been a dwelling in her mind that was larger or brighter—more cheerful. Still, it's what a person needs, four walls and a roof, shelter.

She supplements the graham crackers from McClure's with a festive-looking package of microwave lasagna that was sitting in the freezer. "Isn't this fun?" she says to Noah. "All we have to do is push the button."

Noah stares intently. Behind the window in the glossy white box, plastic wrap and Styrofoam revolve turbulently as intense, artificial smells pour out into the room. Shadows move in Noah's dark eyes, and he turns away.

"What?" she says.

He leans against her leg and says something. She has to bend down to hear.

"Not today. Thumb, Noah," she says as he puts his into his mouth. "No doggies today."

Alma might have thought of canceling her date with Gerry, Kristina thinks. It's been years since the two of them have seen each other, and it would be awfully nice to have some company. But there's Noah to concentrate on, anyhow. She urges him to eat, but he doesn't seem to be hungry. For that matter, neither is she. She spreads a sheet out on the futon that she and Alma dragged from the couch frame onto the floor, and there—she and Noah have their bed.

Outside, the wind is still hurtling clumsily by, thrashing through the branches and low, twiggy growth, groaning and pleading in the language of another world. But she and Noah are hidden under the blankets. She'll turn out the light, the night will be a deep blue swatch, Noah's cold will die down, and in the morning the wind will be gone and the sun will shine. She reaches up to the switch.

The whoosh of darkness brings Eli—surging around her from the four corners of the earth, bursting Alma's tinny little house apart.

She gasps for breath and flings aside the churning covers; she stumbles into the kitchen where she stands naked at the window. A dull splotch of moonlight on the plastic expands and contracts in the wind.

"Kissy?" a tiny, hoarse voice says behind her.

The small form hovers in the shifting darkness. It holds out its arms to be picked up. The blank dark pools of its eye sockets face her.

"Go back to sleep," she says as calmly as she can. Fatigue is making her heart race and stirring up a muddy swirl of worries. Little discomforts and pains are piping up here and there in her body. "Now, please." She turns resolutely away and sits down at the kitchen table. After a few seconds she hears him pad away.

Fortunately, there's an open pack of Alma's cigarettes out on the table. Her hands shake slightly but manage to activate a match. Flame from sulfur, matter into clouds . . .

Everything that happens is out there waiting for you to come to it. One little turn, then another, then another—and by the time you think to wonder where you are and how you got there, it's dark.

She can't see back. It's like looking into a well. She sees her long hair ripple forward. There's nothing in front of her. But then rising up behind her, the moving shadows of trees, of the muddy road, of cars, of faces—Nonie, Roger, Liz, the girls from the distant farms, Eli . . . At the dark center of the water her own face is indistinct.

And then there she is, standing indecisively at the bus station, over a year and a half ago, in the grimy little city where she grew up. She was a whole year out of high school, and there had been nothing but dead-end clubs and drugs, and dead-end jobs. Years before, Alma had told her, go to college, go to college, but when the time came she couldn't see it—the loans and the drudgery to repay them and then what, anyhow. There was talk of modeling—someone she met—but she was too lanky and maybe a little strange for catalog work, it turned out, and too something else for serious fashion. Narrow shoulders, and the wrong attitude, they said; no attitude, apparently. So for a while, instead of putting clothes on for the photos it had been taking them off, and after that it was working in a store that sold shoes and purses.

When she was little there had been moments like promises, disclosures—glimpses of radiant things to come that were so clear and sharp they seemed like erupting memories. A sudden scent, a sudden slant of light, and a blur of pictures would stream past. It was as if she'd been born out of a bright, fragrant world into the soiled, boarded up room of her life. She chose the town for its name from the list of destinations at the bus station.

Soft hills flowed in distant rings around the little country town, and a chick-colored sun shone over it. Out in front of the pretty white houses were bright, round-petaled flowers. Sheep drifted across the meadows like clouds.

Every day she awoke to the white houses and the gentle hills, and it was like looking down at a tender, miniature world. The sky was pure; the planet spun in it brightly, like a marble.

Tourists came on the weekends for the charged air, and the old-fashioned inns. With so many people coming to play, it had been easy to get work.

The White Rabbit . . . with that poor animal, its petrified red glass eyes staring down at her and Nonie from over the bar. It wasn't enough they shot it and stuffed it, Nonie had said; they had to plunk it down right here to listen to Frank's sickening jokes.

A pouty Angora mewed up at them from its cushion near Kristina's ankle. Good thing they didn't call this place The White Cat, huh, you, she'd said, and just then Frank craned into the dining room. Girls—ladies. A lull is not a holiday. A lull is when we wipe down tables, make salads, roll silver . . .

Or The White Guy, Nonie said.

Nonie—all that crazy, crimpy hair—energy crackling right out from it! Her new friend. Nonie had a laugh like little colored blocks of wood toppling.

It wasn't long before she moved into a room in the pretty white house Nonie and Munsen were renting. Nonie was still waiting tables on weekends then, saving up; she was planning to buy a bakery. Nonie and Munsen were hoping to have a baby.

How nice it had been when Munsen came home on his lunch breaks to hang out in the kitchen, and they were all three together. Munsen, looking for all the world like a stoopy plant, draped in the aroma of butter, smiling, blinking behind his gold-rimmed specs, drinking his coffee, sometimes a beer.

And Nonie—that was a sight to see! Little Nonie, slapping the dough around, waking the dormant yeast as if she were officiating at the beginning of the world.

How had Nonie figured out to do that, she'd wanted to know.

No figuring involved, Nonie told her; when she was a kid she was always just sort of rolling around in the flour.

She'd given Kristina a little hug. Never mind, she said. You'll find something to roll around in.

Anyhow, Munsen said, it's overrated.

Sure, Nonie said, but it what?

Munsen had sighed. It all, he said.

One star and then another detached from its place and flamed across the dark. The skies were dense with constellations. Whole galaxies streamed toward the porch where she sat with Nonie and Munsen on her nights off, watching the coded messages from her future, light years away.

She helped, but maybe she slowed things down a bit. Well, she did, though Nonie never would have said. So while Nonie carried on in the kitchen, she would take Nonie's rattly old car and deliver orders of bread and pastries to various inns and restaurants. And Nonie and Munsen let her have her room for free.

Save those pennies! Nonie said.

For what? she had thought; uh-oh.

Every day there were new effects, modulations of colors and light, as if something were being perfected at the core. Going from day to day was like unwrapping the real day from other days made out of splendid, fragile, colored tissue.

———

The tourists started swarming in for the drama of the changing leaves. Every weekend the town bulged with tourists. Someone named Roger took her to dinner on one of her nights off, to The Mill Wheel, where she subbed sometimes.

Roger had waxy, poreless skin, as if he'd spent years packed in a box, and his blue eyes shone with joyous, childlike gluttony, lighting now on booty, now on tribute.

It had come to him, he told her, that it was time to make some changes. He was living in the city—toiling, as he put it, in the engine rooms of finance, but one day not long ago his company had vanished, along with so many others, in a little puff of dirty smoke. What was he to do? His portfolio had been laid waste. So, the point was, he could scrounge for something else, but it had occurred to him, why not just pull up stakes and live in some reasonably gratifying way? There wasn't any money to speak of out there these days, anyhow.

Money to speak of. A different kind of money than the money her mother had counted out for groceries.

So why not look at this period of being broke as an opportunity, he was saying, that might not come again. Because this was, he'd informed her, one's life.

The waiter poured a little wine into Roger's glass. How is that, sir? the waiter said.

Fine, Roger said, very good. He beamed as the waiter poured out a full glass for Kristina.

Thanks, Artie, she said, and Artie had bowed.

You know everyone! Roger observed.

Yeah, well, she knew Artie, unfortunately. A tiny chapter her history would have been better off without.

What is it? Roger asked. He'd smiled quizzically and taken her hand. What are you thinking?

She'd looked at him, smiled back, and withdrawn her hand.

Roger's marriage, for better or worse, had come to its natural end, he was saying. And while he looked for the occasion to make that clear, in a sensitive manner, to his wife, he was scouting out arenas in which to mine his stifled and neglected capacities.

As he talked, he gazed at her raptly, as though she were a mirror. When he reached for his wallet, to show her pictures of his children, she withdrew her hand from his again, and concentrated on drinking the very good wine. By the time they had polished off nearly two bottles and Roger was willing to throw in the towel, The Mill Wheel had almost emptied out, and Artie was lounging at the bar, staring at her evilly.

After that evening, she turned down dinner invitations, and eventually she started wearing a ring. At some point it came to her attention that Roger had indeed moved to town. In fact, he was increasingly to be seen in the afternoons hanging out at one of the bars or another, brainstorming his next move in life with the help of the bartenders.

The brilliant autumn days graded into a dazzling, glassy winter with skies like prisms, and then spring drifted down, as soft as pale linen. She painted her room a deep, mysterious blue.

Where on earth was she going to go if Nonie and Munsen had this baby they kept talking about?

She kept seeing women around her age, or anyway not much older, coming into town in their beat-up cars or pickups, to stock up. They looked sunburned and hardy and ready for the next thing, as if they were climbing out of water after a swim. Big, friendly dogs frisked around them.

Where could they be coming from? From out in the country, of course—way out, from the wild, ramshackle farms, where the weeds shot up and burst into sizzling flowers.

The kitchen is freezing. She goes into the bedroom and selects a worn chenille robe from Alma's closet. Alma's clock, with the big, reproving green numbers, says ten thirty.

So, where is Alma? Way back, when they were growing up almost next door to each other in the projects, and their mothers let Alma exercise her fierce affections on the little girl she knew to be her half-sister, Alma took care of her while their mothers worked.

And young as Kristina was, Alma confided in her. Back then, Kristina felt Alma's suffering over boys like the imprint of a slap on her own skin. Evidently things haven't changed much for Alma, and it's saddening now to picture Alma's history with Gerry: the big guy on the next bar stool, a few annihilating hours of alcohol, a messy, urgent interval at his place or hers, the sequence recapitulated now and again—an uneasy companionability hemmed about with recriminations and contingencies . . .

In her peripheral vision, Eli appears.

It was busy, and she didn't get a good look at him right away, but even at the other end of the room, sitting and talking to Frank, he was conspicuous, as if he were surrounded by his own splendid night.

Yes. She'd felt the active density right away, the gravitational pull.

It must have been several weeks later that he was there again with Frank. And when Frank got up to strut, and sniff around for mistakes, Eli looked right at her over Frank's shoulder and smiled—not the usual sort of stranger's smile, like a fence marking a divide. Not a stranger's smile at all.

It was a Friday night; the tourists started to pour in, and when she had a chance to peek back at him he was gone. He didn't reappear.

Then one night she glanced up from the table where she was taking an order and he was sitting at the bar. A little shock rippled through her. Evidently she'd been waiting.

He was looking for Frank again of course, but, as she explained, it was Frank's night off. Too bad you didn't call first, she said.

No phone, he told her, lightly.

No phone. Okay, but how did he find people when he wanted to?

Finding people is easy, he'd said; it's not getting found that's hard.

It was a slow evening, and early. They stood side by side at the bar. She could feel his gaze; she let herself float on it. How long had he and Frank been friends, she'd asked.

He'd seemed amused. Strictly business, he said. And what about her? Who was she? Where was she from?

As she spoke, he looked at her consideringly, and sorrow rose up, closing over her. How little she had to show for her eighteen years on the planet! In an hour or so the room would be filled with frenetic diners, killing time until it killed them. They might as well be shot and stuffed themselves.

I don't know about this town, though, she'd said. I'm starting to feel like I'm asleep.

So, maybe you need your sleep, he said. This isn't a bad place for a nap. Why not nap? Soon you'll be refreshed and ready to move on out.

She took to sitting at her window. Haze covered the hills in the distance; the sky had become opaque, and close. Where had that real day gone?

Sometimes after she finished delivering the orders in Nonie's old car she'd just drive around, down the small highways to the shady dirt roads. Sometimes she thought she'd caught a glimpse of Eli in town, just rounding a corner, disappearing through a doorway; she wasn't well, she thought—it seemed that maybe she never had been.

Maybe I'll try to find myself a place out in the country, she told Nonie, and get my own car.

That would be great, Nonie said. I'll help you look, if you want.

Wouldn't you even miss me? she'd said.

Of course, Nonie said. But you wouldn't be far. You'd come see us all the time.

And I'd keep helping you, she'd said.

And you'd keep helping me, Nonie said.

She can still see in perfect detail Zoe's face as she saw it in the The White Rabbit, for the first and only time. Truly she could only have glimpsed it—in profile as Zoe and Eli left, or in the mirror over the bar—but she might as well have scrutinized it for hours. It's almost as if she had been inside Zoe, looking into that mirror over the bar herself, seeing herself in the perfect dark skin, the perfect head, her hair almost shorn. She can feel Zoe's delicate body working as if it were her own, and she can feel the weight of the sleeping baby strapped to Zoe's back.

The lovely face with its long, wide-set eyes floats in Alma's plastic-covered window now, unsmiling, distant.

Eli had waved as he and Zoe left, but it was as if she was watching him from behind dark glass; she didn't wave back, or smile.

And Zoe appeared not to have seen her. The fact is, Zoe appeared not to see anything at all; Zoe had looked unearthly and singular, as if she were a blind woman.

Nonie was five months pregnant by the time she and Munsen told Kristina. She was superstitious, she said, and she'd had trouble before. She chuckled and patted her stomach. But this is getting pretty obvious, she said. I figured you were just being polite.

For months Munsen and Nonie had been aware there was a baby in the house.

Oh, her blue room! It had been pretty poor comfort that day.

Of course, it hadn't really been her room for the five previous months.

And the lady at the real estate office! Irritably raking back the streaky hair, the rectangular glasses in their thin frames, the expectant expression that went blank when Kristina spoke, or changed to a hurried smile . . .

A little less than fifteen hundred dollars! Every penny she'd saved. Not quite enough, was it, even for some crumbling hut out there, all made out of candy.

While Nonie baked rolls and Munsen sanded down to satin the cradle he'd built for the invisible baby, she'd flipped through Munsen's atlas. Chicago, Maine, Seattle, Atlanta—or why not go to one of those places really far away, where people spoke languages she couldn't understand at all? Because that was the point—this direction or that—apparently it didn't matter where she went.

The end of summer was already sweeping through town, hectic with color and heat, as if it were making a desperate stand against the darkness and cold ahead. Nearly a year had passed.

He was watching her as she walked right by him at the bar. Hey, he said, and held his hand out. No handshakes? No greetings, no how are yous, none of the customary effusions?

She had blushed deeply; she shook her hair back. All right, she said, greetings.

She remembers standing there, waiting for the blush to calm while he stretched lazily.

Well, since you ask, he'd said, here's the data. A lot of travel, recently, a lot of work. And my girlfriend is gone.

It was as if there were other words inside those, in the way there are with jokes. That's too bad, she said.

Why, exactly? he said, and the mortifying blush flared again.

To tell you the truth, he was saying, it was obvious almost from the beginning that there were going to be problems.

That woman had looked like someone with problems, she remembers having thought; that woman in the mirror looked like she was drifting there between the land of the living and the land of the dead.

And what was she up to herself these days, he'd wanted to know.

She took a deep breath to establish some poise in her thoughts. Since you ask, she said, I think nap time is just about up for me.

That very night, when she got back after work, he was there in the kitchen. He and Munsen were drinking beer, and he must have just finished saying something that made Nonie and Munsen laugh. She'd stood in the doorway, silenced.

There she is, Nonie said. How come you never brought this guy around? He's okay.

Guess I don't need to introduce anyone, she'd said.

Nonie and Munsen were sitting at the table, but he was lounging against the wall, looking at her, not quite smiling. It seemed I might not have a whole lot of time, he said. So I thought I'd drop on by to ask for your hand.

He waited for her to approach. She couldn't feel herself moving. She laughed a little, breathlessly, as he removed her ring, looking at her. Dollar store, she said, and he dropped it into the ashtray on the kitchen table.

Wow! Munsen said. Okay!

There's some stuff I have to deal with tonight, Eli said. Sit tight. I'll be back in for you at noon.

Roger was already at the bar of The White Rabbit when she went in to leave a note for Frank the next morning. His arm was around one of the new waitresses. His wife and kids were where by then, she wondered. Probably living in his abandoned SUV on just the same street where she and Alma grew up, all those years ago. Hey, she'd said. Hey, he said cheerfully. Actually, he hadn't seemed to quite remember who she was.

Wear something pretty, Eli had said the night before as he left, and so she was wearing her favorite dress, with its little straps and bare back. Her hair was pinned up. He swung her satchel into the back of the truck and then they climbed in.

Beyond the windshield, the hills had an arresting, detailed look. Red and gold were beginning to edge into the leaves. The hills were like inverted bowls or gentle cones, covered with trees. She had the impression that she could see each and every tree. The trees, like the hills, were shaped like gentle cones or inverted bowls. Would you look at that, she said.

Huh, he said, that's right. A nice little volumetric exercise.

He reached over and unpinned her hair.

This is a very crazy thing to do, she said.

Which is crazier? he said. This, or not this?

She must have been smiling, because he'd laughed. What a skeptic, he'd said. So, it's a risk, yes? Okay, but a risk of what? Look, here's the alternative, we meet, we like each other, we say hello, we say goodbye. Now there's an *actual* risk. That's pure recklessness. We're scared—is that so bad? Because when you're scared, you can be pretty sure you're on to something.

She remembers a sudden, panicked sensation that something was wrong, and then all her relief because it was only the ring—she wasn't wearing her dime store ring.

It's pretty clear, he was saying, the things people know about each other in an instant are the important things. But all right, let's say the important things aren't everything. Let's say the unimportant things count, too—even a lot. The point is, though, we can spend as long as we like learning those unimportant things about each other. We can spend years, if we want, or we can spend a few hours. If you want, I can bring you back here tomorrow. We can say goodbye now, if you want.

They watched each other, smiling faintly. The silence raced through her over and over.

Say the word, he'd told her, and you're back where you were.

Past the gorge, where she went to swim sometimes with Nonie and Munsen, past the old foundry, past the quarry, the hills flowing around them, mile after mile, so little traffic on the highway, the sweet air pouring by and the sun ringing through the sky like trumpets. Then they were in the woods, among the woven streamers of sunlight and shadow. The dirt road was studded with rocks, and grooved, tossing her around as if she were on the high seas.

None of her drives in Nonie's car had taken her in that direction, or nearly that far. There were no other people to be seen. Every leaf and twig signified, like a sound, or a letter of the alphabet.

By the way, she said, how did you know where to look for me last night?

Hey, he said. In a town that size?

———

Light brimmed and quivered through the leaves in trembling drops. All around was a faint, high, glittering sound. The cabin was a maze of light and shadow—all logs, with polished plank floors, and porches. And with the attic and lofts and little ladders and stairs, you hardly knew whether you were inside or up in a tree house.

There was running water, and there was even electricity, which he used mainly for the washing machine and the big freezer at the back. He brought her out past a group of sheds to the vegetable garden he'd been clearing and tending, and to the shiny little creek. If you walked into the woods, within just a couple of minutes you couldn't even see the cabin. When the sun began to set they came back, and he showed her how to light the kerosene lanterns and the temperamental little dragon of a stove.

There was a lot of game in the freezer, Eli said; hunters often gave him things. But he'd kept it simple tonight—for all he knew, she might be the fainthearted sort.

He had opened a bottle of rich red wine and they ate wonderful noodles, with mushrooms from the woods and herbs, and a salad from the garden. He watched, with evident satisfaction, her astonishment at the bright, living flavors.

You have to live like this to taste anything like this, he said. Streamline yourself. Clear away the junk. Prepare for an encounter.

But anyhow, she'd said, and in the stillness she'd felt like a dancer, balancing—I'm not fainthearted.

How on earth was she accounting in those first hours, she wonders now, for the baby she had seen at the bar with Eli?

Well, if she'd thought of too many questions out front, she'd probably still be rotting away in that little town, living in somebody's spare room. She'd been in no position at that moment to be thinking of the sort of questions whose answers are, Go back to sleep.

They were finishing off the bottle of wine when he explained that his partner Hollis and Hollis's girlfriend, Liz, were taking care of Noah right now, as they did from time to time. It was all kind of improvisational, not ideal, but Zoe had been erratic and moody, so anyhow it was an improvement over that situation.

He rested his hand on her neck, and stars shot from it. If it had been up to her, the dishes would have stayed in the sink till morning—till winter. But Eli just held her against him for a blinding moment. Here's some of that new stuff to learn about me, he said. I am very, very disciplined.

And what had she been dreaming about that first morning? She was hidden behind something. Something was about to happen to someone very far away, who was her. There were showers of burning debris. The noise that woke her came into the dream as an alarm, she thinks, but it all dissolved like a screen over the morning light, and there was Eli lying next to her, his eyes still closed, shadows of leaves moving across him like a rich, patterned cloak.

A mechanical growl was pushing through the racket of birds and leaves. She peered out and a mottled green truck came into view. The sun must have been up for some time—it was so bright! The door of the truck slammed, and Eli groaned. Hollis, he said, and opened his eyes.

She wrapped herself around him, but he kissed her, untangled himself, and drew his jeans on. There were dogs barking. Powder! T-bone! someone yelled. Down!

Well, they're here, Eli said, and tossed her dress to her.

She'd watched from the top of the stairs as Liz transferred the baby over to him. The baby whimpered, and Eli put him on his shoulders.

A cigarette dangled from Hollis's mouth, and a line of smoke swayed up past his gray eyes. Would you mind kindly keeping that shit out of the house, please? Eli said. And away from my kid in general?

Hollis pinched the cigarette out with his fingers and flicked it through the door. So how about some coffee? he said.

The dogs were milling and bumping at things. Don't rush me, don't rush me, Eli said. He stretched, then, and reached over to tousle Hollis's floppy brown hair. I just got up.

Hollis inclined his head. Impressive, he said. Outstanding.

They'd looked like a tribe, Hollis and Liz and Eli, tall and slouchy and elastic. She sat on the stairs, rags of her dream still clinging to her, until he called for her.

It was Hollis who tracked down the guns and kept on top of the orders and sales. Because this guy's too pure in heart to have a computer in his place, Hollis had said, tilting back to appraise her.

No phone line, Eli said, unruffled.

My point, Hollis said to her. So I'm stuck with it. He shook his head. Too fucking poetic, this guy.

You are so jealous, Liz told Hollis, sliding her hand inside the back of his jeans.

The good weather continued, and there was the garden and clearing away the persistent brush. There was plenty else, too,

—cleaning, and dealing with the wood for the stove, and endless laundry.

Mostly, of course, there was Noah. Eli was doing a lot of things to the cabin, and the wood chips and splinters and chemicals were flying around everywhere. And there were always tools, and work on the guns going on in the sheds.

You've really got to watch him every second, Eli said. And I mean every second.

It was true; if she turned around for a *second* he'd have gotten himself over to the stove or the door or a pail of something. So she watched and she watched. But at night, when Noah was asleep, she had Eli to herself and that was well worth the trouble of the day, and more.

Usually, it was he who cooked. Sometimes just vegetables, but sometimes rabbit or venison or little birds. Often, as evening came, the sky turned greenish—a dissipating, regretful color.

She remembers his voice coming through that color from outside, asking her to get the stove going. But when he came in almost a half an hour later, she hadn't managed. I'm sorry, she said. How tired she used to get, back at the beginning! And she'd actually started to cry.

He looked at her and sighed. Here, he said. I'll show you again.

Sometimes the woods shook and flared with thunder and lightning. The deer came crashing through the trees. Way down in the valley the little foxes jumped straight up from the grass. Sometimes, walking near the creek with Eli, Noah on his shoulders or back, she would hear just a little whisper or rustle somewhere, or there would be a streak in the corner of her eye. Are there snakes? she asked.

He folded his arms around her and explored her ear with his tongue. Not to worry. They won't bother you unless you do something to stir them up.

At first Noah would go rigid when she tried to hold him. He'd swat at her if she bent down for him, and he'd scream when it seemed he thought Eli was in earshot.

And then Eli had to come in from outside and hold him or swing him around while she looked on. There we go, Eli would say when Noah calmed down. And sometimes he'd go back out hardly looking at her.

Noah was still only a baby then, but every day he was looking more like a little boy; every day he figured out new ways to resist and defeat her.

Just pick him up like a big ham, Eli said. Look. Like this, right, Noah?

He smiled at her as he went out, but later he'd taken her by the shoulders and looked at her very seriously. I know it's hard, he said. But you've got to start taking some more responsibility around here. She averted her face as he leaned over to kiss her; she'd just sneaked a cigarette.

It was early on that they talked about Zoe. She wasn't ready, Eli said; it wasn't her fault. In fact, there was a lot that was his fault, really a lot, he hated to think about it. But anyhow, it was just the way she was constituted—she lacked courage. She was always dissatisfied. And she always would be, because she didn't have the courage to face the fact that what happens to you is largely of your own choosing.

He turned back, then, to whatever it was he'd been doing. But she was still listening, she remembers; something was still flickering in what he'd said.

Does she want to see Noah? She'd asked after a moment.

That's not a possibility, he said. His back was to her.

She was willing to leave her kid, he said. And that one's on her.

Noah isn't sounding so good. She can hear him snuffling from the kitchen. She goes to check. He's a bit sweaty—maybe Alma's right, that he's got a little fever. But little kids get sick all the time. Anyhow, what makes Alma the authority? The hospital she works at is for crazy people, not for little kids.

Tomorrow she'll get him some kind of treat—a fuzzy doggie toy, maybe. Or something. Not that there's money to burn.

She remembers once trying chocolate syrup in his milk, trying a story, promising maybe a trip into town later with Eli, but Noah still whining and crying hour after hour. All right, that's it, you behave now, she'd said. Or you're going right in your crib and you're not going to be seeing that bottle of yours anytime soon.

He let out a little yelp of fury.

Fine, then, scream, she said. Go ahead and scream. Just cry until you melt yourself away for all I care. You know he's not going to hear you out there over all that noise. They'd stared at each other. He is not going to hear you.

She turned away from him and opened one of Eli's books. When she glanced back Noah was still standing there, looking at her. What? she said.

He'd wobbled for a moment on his feet, and then plopped down on his rear end, crying again.

Eli went into town to get supplies and took Noah with him. To give her a break, he said.

She'd listened to the truck heaving itself out on the rutted road. It was the first time she'd been truly alone in the cabin for more than a few minutes. Sunlight and silence shimmered down through the leaves all around it. In the sparkling dimness the floor shone like a lake. All around her there was a tingling quiet. She shivered, then sat very still, to enter it.

It was like a garden, or park, that opened out forever. Peaceful, clever animals, invisible in the abundence, paused to take note of her. She had found her way, through patience and good fortune.

How's it been going—Eli said, when he returned, looking around at the cabin. She'd finished the dishes and tidied up. — Any lions or tigers?

Hollis's green truck pulled up, waking her. The sheets still noted Eli's place, but they were cold. She'd watched from a window upstairs. The dogs were huffing and circling in back, and Hollis and Liz got out. Eli was carrying Noah. He handed Noah over to Liz. He called something up to Kristina, and then he and Hollis got into Eli's truck and pulled back out onto the dirt road.

She heard Liz downstairs with Noah. After a while she

came down herself. Hi, Liz said. Eli told me you might want some help with Noah today.

Oh, thanks, she'd said. But we'll be fine.

That's okay, Liz said, flopping herself down on the couch. Just toss me out when you get sick of me.

Sorry not to have given you a heads-up, Eli said later. But we had an unexpected opportunity. To do an errand for your old pal, Frank.

Frank, she said. What did Frank want?

He's into Mausers these days, I'm sorry to tell you. He had his tender heart set on a 1944 Kreigsmodell, and we just happened to come across one at a reasonable price. Oh, give me the sweet old American revolver guys any day. Or the Derringer guys, or the Winchester guys. Anyone at all—the Finnish military model guys. I've got to admit it's not necessarily a super high IQ clientele, but Frank is special. It's amazing he hasn't already blown his brains out by mistake.

Frank! To think of the way that freak had gotten her to scurry around. Like a rabbit! She'd let out a little whoop.

What, Eli said. Oh, right—like how would anyone know if he had.

I don't really need Liz to come help, she said the next time he'd had to go off for the day.

He'd looked at her. It doesn't hurt to have reinforcements, he said. And I'll have her bring any stuff you might need from town.

———

The leaves were truly turning when she first went back into town with Eli. The cycle of the year had locked tight, but she'd slipped out in time.

Past the quarry and the foundry and the gorge, into the painted, prissy town. She'd lived there only months ago, and yet it didn't look like a real place any longer—it just looked like a picture of a place.

She cast her mind back and saw Zoe—the way Zoe had looked carrying Noah, gliding and regal.

Want me to carry you? she said. Noah protested, but Eli slung him onto her back.

He was heavy, and she had to cede him to Eli pretty soon, but for a while as they went about their errands, buying food and batteries and seeds, she felt, in the weight of him, her elevated station. And when they went to the diner for lunch, people she had barely spoken to in the old days came over to admire him.

They went to one of the fancy tourist stores, and Eli picked out two dresses for her. Back in the truck, with Noah settled on her lap, she felt in the bag at the slippy, lovely fabric.

Anything you particularly want to do before we head home? Eli said.

Home. The way she had lived at Nonie and Munsen's— like a little animal! I bet Nonie and Munsen would enjoy seeing Noah, she said.

Are you saying you'd like to stop by there now? he said.

She'd glanced at him, then shrugged. We're here.

He was looking at her steadily. Do you want to see them? It's been awhile, she said.

All you have to say, he said. All you have to say is that you'd like to see them.

But neither Munsen's car nor Nonie's was out in front. Well, too bad, Eli said.

Eli had so many books. How nice it had been to take them down from the shelves and look at them. In the one about the ocean, the prettiest fish imaginable hovered so weightlessly you could almost see them moving—rising, lingering, darting down with the flick of a tail. And the gorgeous plants and flowers around them were really other animals.

How did he get out? Eli was saying. He was in front of her, holding his machete in one hand and Noah by the other, and rage was flashing off him in sheets, like lightning. *It was just luck I didn't kill him with this.*

She was still shaking when Eli returned outside. She could hardly stand. Her hand was clamped around Noah's shoulder. If you want something you come to me, do you hear? she told him, her voice tight. You come to me. You do not go outside to bother your father. Try some stunt like that again and I'll— I don't know what I'll do—

On rainy days when Eli wasn't working, she curled up against him while he read out loud. Noah curled up at his other side, or played quietly nearby. Eli read from books about history or animals or the earth and other planets. The world was living and breathing, each bit in its place. When the weather was good the three of them played together in the woods.

Whenever Eli went away for the day, Liz came in her pickup, and stayed on and on. Noah would go rigid with joy when the big, patient dogs, with their amazing tails and fur and tongues came huffling toward him through the door, but Kristina set herself to endure some bad hours.

Sometimes for days afterward, Kristina felt like a swan that had gotten caught in an oil slick—sticky and polluted, not fit to be near Eli. How could he deal with Liz? Her loudness, her opinions about every pointless thing, her gossipy chattering, the way she made everything ordinary . . . Eli had shrugged: she was an old, old friend, there was a lot of history, she was as loyal as a person could be . . .

Noah was making his way toward them, holding his empty bottle. Hey, Noah— Liz said. You're really getting that locomotion thing down! Wow, I can't believe how fast he's growing, look at him. Noah! she grabbed him up and tickled him, blowing hard into his hair.

Kristina remembers watching as Noah exploded into giggles.

Does he still cry for Zoe all the time? Liz said, when Noah had run back to the dogs.

For Zoe? she'd said.

Wow, it used to be Mama, Mama, Mama the whole fucking time, Liz said. Poor little sweetie. It used to drive Eli nuts.

I guess he's forgotten about her, she'd said.

That's great, good for you, she was a major pain, if you ask me, Liz had said, Miss Too Gorgeous for this World. I always felt like smacking her myself, to tell you the truth. She didn't appreciate what she had in Eli. Eli's intense, so what? He's got his own way of looking at things. He's more evolved than other people. Plus, he gave her everything. He was fucking great to her, and he put up with her shit a long, long time before he even *began* to lose patience. Liz was holding one of the dish towels, creasing it absently and fiercely.

They've been gone so long, Kristina remembers saying. Did they say when they were planning to get back?

Oh, you never know with those two, Liz said. She tossed the towel onto the table. They take their time with the custom work. Of course that's why they've got such a great reputation, obviously. Hollis can find just about anything, and Eli can convert just about anything. He's got great hands. She pushed her hair back and eased a pack of cigarettes from her pocket. Great, great hands. . . . She lit a cigarette and inhaled, closing her eyes.

Kristina watched her for a while. Liz— she'd said, and her voice came out fuzzy. Can I take one of those?

Help yourself. Liz opened her eyes; she'd sounded almost angry. I won't tell.

The next time Eli and Hollis went off, Noah played happily with the dogs while Liz talked on, but then suddenly Liz exclaimed, and put her hands to her forehead.

Are you okay? Kristina asked.

Sorry, Liz said. I've been getting these crucifying migraines.

Do you want to lie down? she'd asked. Then her breath caught for a moment. Do you want to leave?

Would you mind? Liz said. You don't have to mention to Eli it was so early, though. But if I don't get out of here fast, basically, I'm not going to be able to drive till probably tomorrow.

That afternoon, with Liz and the dogs gone so early, no matter how often Kristina explained that Eli was coming back soon, Noah cried and fussed, swatting at her with his little hands.

You'd be less cranky if you ate something, she said. What about some applesauce?

No, Noah said.

Well, then, a graham cracker. Don't you like your graham crackers anymore?

No, he said.

Such a tiny word. Such a tiny voice.

Do you know how furious your father's going to be if I have to tell him you refused to eat one single thing all day? Do you know how angry he's going to be with you? Are you going to make me tell him?

He looked at her, swaying a bit on his feet. Bad Kissy, he said.

Not bad me, bad you! Bad you! Do you want me to smack you? Because I'm just about ready to.

Bad Kissy, he said. Bad Kissy.

Don't you talk to me like that! Don't you look at me like that! Do you think I like picking up after you all day? And getting you your food when you do deign to eat? And cleaning up all your mess? I know you don't like having me around. And do you know what? I think I've just about had it with you! One more sassy word and I'm going to walk right out that door, and you'll just have to take care of yourself. Now, you eat your graham cracker this minute, or I'm out of here.

But then he was screaming and kicking and banging his head against the wall.

It was the moment; it was their chance, and thank God she'd recognized that. But just remembering the struggle, she starts to sweat—scooping him up and trying to hold him still, and all the time he was kicking at her and screaming. And clinging to her so fiercely she could hardly get him over to the sofa to sit down with him.

It must have been over an hour that she was holding on to him before he was calm enough for her to speak. All right then, Noah, she said.

He had gone limp. She held him steadily on her lap and broke the graham cracker in half. She wouldn't let him avoid her eyes.

I'm not going to leave you alone, she said. Listen to me. This is a promise. I am not going to leave you alone.

Tears were still rolling down his cheeks, and he hiccuped.

They watched each other as she ate her half of the cracker. She nodded, and held the other half of the cracker out to him. Slowly, gulping back the last of his sobs, still watching her, he chewed it laboriously down.

When Eli returned, Noah was still in her lap, asleep. Where's Liz? he said.

You just missed her, she said.

Huh, Eli said. And this one—trouble?

She rested her cheek against Noah's springy hair and tightened her hold on him for a moment before handing him over. No, she said. No trouble.

The cold came and kept them frequently inside. Eli was working in the shed a lot, and from time to time he'd have to take a trip or go to a show with Hollis. When they were away, Liz arrived for the daylight hours. When her truck finally pulled away, darkness folded in over the cabin.

———

When Eli was home, he was quiet. He read to Noah, and when he grew tired of it he turned to his own reading. He was looking a little pale, she'd thought. Eli? she said.

What's that? he'd said, pausing on his way up to the loft.

She shook her head: nothing.

Noah pined and clamored for his friends the dogs. Shh, she told him, and took him where he could play without disturbing Eli.

Once in a while a car would pull up, and some man or other would get out and Eli would take him around back to the sheds. She stayed upstairs then with Noah.

While Noah played with the blocks Eli had made him, she watched out the window as the men returned to their trucks or cars and headed off to the hills, or the hills beyond them, or the hills and cities beyond those—glinting pins springing up on the map.

And she watched Noah as he concerned himself with the blocks or with his crayons. Playing, it was called—the deep, sweet concentration, the massive effort to familiarize himself with the things of the world. Can she remember that, being so little herself, being so lost? Probably Alma had already been around, looking out for her, but she can't find a trace of that time in her mind. It was her basis, and yet it was gone.

Want me to carry you? she'd ask, and he'd raise up his little arms to her. She held him as he woke from his naps, and felt the damp heat coming off his gold skin and little ringlets. He snuggled against her, and in an attic dark area of her sleeping thoughts, things clarified for a moment, and aligned.

He never fussed anymore. He had made his choice; he had forgotten.

Sometimes Kristina felt Zoe hovering nearby, drawn by

her need, watching along with her as Noah played. But Noah never even looked up.

Yes, he had surely forgotten. Poor little thing—he was a prisoner.

Are you not talking to me? Eli said one day.

Not talking to you? she said. She looked up. He was sitting across the room, looking at her. The book he'd been reading was closed, resting on his lap.

You don't seem to be talking to me.

You were reading, she said.

Now I'm not reading, he said.

She looked at him for a clue. Is there something you want me to talk about?

He sighed and opened his book again, but a moment later he looked up at her again. You're happy, he said.

Yes, she said. He seemed to be gazing back at her sadly from some time in the future. I'm happy.

Well, good, then. He walked over to her and stroked the back of her neck, looking at her thoughtfully. He kissed her temple and then he returned to his book.

He picked up some yeast for her in town. She baked bread the way Nonie had showed her to, and the companionable aroma brought Nonie to visit.

She remembers the way she imagined showing Nonie around the cabin. It was as if she were unfolding it and spreading it out flat, like a map, so she could see all of it at once herself.

———

How's Eli these days? Liz said.

Fine, she'd said.

Well, I'm glad one of them is keeping it together, Liz said. Hollis is fried. But everything always happens all at once, doesn't it.

I guess, Kristina had said.

Well, but I mean what kind of dickhead doesn't back up the files? Liz said. I guess that genius they found, I hate to think where, is still saying he can resurrect the hard drive, but who believes that's going to happen? And anyhow, who cares, it's the thing with that Coffield lunatic, obviously, that's really putting him around the bend.

Yes? Kristina said. The room darkened for a moment, and she'd sat down.

Well, it's sure getting enough attention. Eli must have told you. You literally can't turn on the TV for one second without seeing the pictures. God, those kids must have been cute! With that red hair?

Kristina had let out a little sound.

But they don't usually go after the source, Liz said. Unless like it's a kid putting holes in his parents or at school, something like that. And anyhow, according to Hollis for whatever that's worth, he did check the guy out, and there was no history.

Sleet coated the trees and power lines, and froze. For a day or two the woods were shining glass, and the branches snapped and fell under the weight of the ice. Nights were mostly bundled up in silence; you could hear the world breathing in its sleep. When she closed her eyes, she'd see the animals outside in the stark, brilliant moonlight, huddled, or wandering for food—the foxes and the deer, the badgers and the possums and the pretty black bear. The stars overhead contracted in the cold. From bed she could watch them oscillating with intensi-fied light, as if they were about to burst into sharp, glittering fragments.

Is everything all right? she asked him.

Fine, he said.

Can I help with anything?

Can you help? he said. Can you do a conversion with a broken drill press on a 1911 automatic while some drooling trog breathes down your neck?

She went into town with him, and when they passed the old house, both cars were out front. Would you like to drop by? he asked.

I don't really care, she said.

It might be nice for you, he said. You probably miss your friends.

She reached over and stroked his beautiful hair. He could drop her and Noah off, she suggested, while he did errands.

We're in no rush, he said. I'll go in with you.

Nonie was practically a sphere. She greeted Kristina with a little shriek of joy, and cried a bit.

How fussy the kitchen looked to Kristina now, with its shiny appliances and painted walls.

Nonie cut up pieces of her bread with homemade jam for everyone, and Munsen took a couple of beers from the fridge. Eli? he said.

No, thanks, Eli said.

Kristina?

Not for me, either, Munsen—thanks.

Munsen put one bottle back and opened the other for himself. Well, better a full bottle in front of me than a prefrontal lobotomy, he said, ruefully. Then he set Noah on his lap, and while Nonie recounted goings on at The White Rabbit, which were exactly the same old thing, it seemed, Munsen told Noah the true-life adventures of a lonely bottle of beer.

What a fuss Nonie made over Noah! He's going to have a friend, soon, she said.

Kristina had glanced at Eli. He was standing, leaning against the door with his head bowed.

Nonie gave Noah one of the soft little rag dolls she'd made for her own baby, with a little plastic ring in its navel. Noah looked at it with great seriousness, and then rubbed it against his cheek. He looked up at Nonie, who laughed happily and knelt down to give him a squeeze.

So little real time had passed, but she might as well have spent it living at the bottom of the sea with its creaturely landscape, or on the white polar tundras. And all the while Nonie and Munsen had been confined to the little painted town. Goodbye, she thought. Goodbye.

They had almost reached the cabin when Eli finally spoke. That is one inane guy, he said. I wonder how your friend can stand having him around.

The next morning, Kristina couldn't find Noah's new rag doll anywhere.

She was searching through a heap of laundry for it when she realized Eli was in the doorway, watching her. Everything okay? he said.

She turned and they looked at one another. Fine, she said.

Look, I've got to go away tomorrow for a few days, Eli said. But Liz will come over during the days and help.

Eli, she said.

What?

Eli, she said again.

What? he said. Speak to me.

Do you have to go?

Yes, he said. Obviously. Yes, I have to go.

Eli, can't I come with you?

And do what with him?

Bring him along. Can't we come?

No, you cannot come.

Why not?

Why not? It goes without saying why not.

She was twisting one of Noah's little T-shirts in her hands, she realized. But maybe I could be helpful.

Maybe you could, he said. Maybe you could bring a little sunshine into the lives of some lonely gun collectors.

She looked at him, but he was sealed up tight. But don't send Liz at least, please.

Fine, he said. No Liz. And you'll do what for food? You'll do what if you need something? You don't have a phone. You don't have a car.

If you're worried about us, we could go stay with Nonie and Munsen.

With Nonie and Munsen, he said. Would you be happier there?

It's just— she was saying, and then all she really remembers is her surprise, as if his fists were a brand-new part of his body.

A little blood was coming from somewhere; she'd felt something on her face, then checked her hand. There was some blood in her mouth, too. Was that tooth going to come out? she'd wondered idly.

She heard the bare branches clacking together outside in a slight breeze. Then he picked her up from where she'd fallen back.

She remembers Noah's eyes, enormous and blurry-looking. He was sucking at his blanket as Eli carried her upstairs.

He postponed his trip for a few days and stayed with her, curled up next to her in the loft, holding her hands, looking through his books with her. He taught her the names of all the little birds that lived in the leaves around them. He brought her meals on a tray. Noah played quietly downstairs, and sometimes Eli brought him up to be with her. He'd wake her urgently in the night, and after they made love, he kissed her ankles, her toes, her fingertips. Whatever barrier had been between them was gone now, completely.

She stroked his thick, coarse hair. She can feel it under her hand now—almost feel it. Sometimes as he slept she ran her hands over his beautiful face. Poor Eli. He lived with danger all the time.

It wasn't long before the swelling went way down, and she could get around pretty comfortably, as well. The day he left, she found a tube of makeup out on the bureau. Evidently he'd picked it up in town, for the bruises.

She's sure there were marks but nothing too conspicuous by the time she'd finished applying it. She watched carefully for

Liz's expression when she opened the door in her sunglasses.

She's reviewed it so often she's worn away the original, but she knows perfectly well what it was.

She saw Liz register the sunglasses, the masked bruises. She saw Liz politely covering her surprise. And then she saw the thing that she had hoped so fervently that she would not see: she saw that Liz was not very surprised at all.

What did they talk about that morning? Not Eli, that's for sure. Or Hollis, or themselves. They did not, of course, allude to Zoe, though Kristina felt Zoe's volatile essence, as a slight trembling in the air. Eventually, she remembers, Liz began leafing through some trashy magazine she'd brought in with her and paused to study the picture of two pretty faces, empty of anything except a pitiful falseness. They broke up! she exclaimed, looking up at Kristina. Can you believe it? How sad is that!

It was the next day—the second of the three he was to be gone—that Zoe's sorrowing angel spirit passed her hand across Liz's brow, and Liz winced, pressing her hand to her eyes.

And there it was. The opportunity that was as clear as a command. For a moment Kristina had just stood there.

Migraine? she had asked then quietly. Want to go home and lie down?

It was a hard trip into town, and of course you always had to worry about who it was who would stop. But thank heavens it wasn't raining, at least. Feel better, she'd called to Liz, waving from the door as the pickup pulled out, and then as fast as humanly possible, she'd thrown a few necessities for Noah and a change of clothing for herself into her satchel. It wasn't heavy, but progress down the muddy road out to the highway was arduous; something in her side still hurt a lot when she tried to carry Noah.

Hey, it's you, Nonie said when she opened the door. And then her smile was gone. Wuh! Take off those sunglasses for a moment, girl.

Noah let himself be transferred over, and clung to Nonie as she put juice into a bottle for him. Come see the baby, she said.

The baby was red and gummy. Could Noah ever have looked like that? That's incredible, Kristina said.

So, could Nonie and Munsen manage with one car, she'd asked? She could give them over a thousand dollars for Nonie's. She hadn't spent so much as a dime the whole time she'd been with Eli, she realized; he'd taken care of her completely.

Well, you could pay me down the line somewhere, Nonie said. But I'm not really sure I want to know you've got it, if you see what I mean.

That was a good point.

I guess you could report it stolen, Kristina had said. But maybe not for a while? And I guess I'll have to figure out about changing the plates . . .

They'd looked at each other, frowning. Damn, Nonie said. You'd think a person would know how to steal her own car.

And for just a moment, Kristina remembered the way she'd felt sitting around that kitchen in the old days.

Dull moonlight sloshes around like rainwater in the plastic over the window. Alma hasn't come in yet. But Kristina's just as glad to have had this time with Eli.

This afternoon, when Alma answered the door she looked silently for a moment at Kristina, with her bruises and the beautiful, dark child. Then she stood aside to let them in. Heaven knows what she thinks—she didn't ask questions.

When Kristina was young she idolized Alma. It was Alma who looked out for her, and she never doubted for a moment that Alma would gladly take her in if the time came. It hardly matters now that it seems not to be the case. She looks around at Alma's cheap, carelessly ugly place—home for nobody, really. Oh, those shining floors, that quiet, the breathing shadows! Will she ever see it again?

Noah coughs raspily in his sleep. She puts her hand to his hot forehead, and he opens his eyes, just for a moment.

Stolen car! Kidnapped child! How can those words mean her? The deer come crashing through the woods, Zoe holds her breath, Eli's rage is all around them, the red net casting wide. What's right outside? Keys hanging from the warden's belt? The men with the guns? Just guns, or guns and badges . . .

No one looks at anyone—really completely looks—the way he looked at her. She never imagined, or even dared hope, that she would meet such a man or have such a time in her life. Better keep moving. New names, new histories, a nondescript room in a busy city where she'll be able to lose herself and Noah. Watching, hiding, running—that way at least she'll be with Eli for good.

Hi, Barbara, I said. You're Barbara?

Eileen, said the nurse who answered the door. Nights.

I'm the granddaughter, I said.

I figured, Eileen said. Barbara told me you'd be showing up. So where's that handsome brother of yours?

Bill? I said, I beat Bill? That's a first.

Traffic must be bad, she said.

Traffic, traffic . . . I was goggling past Eileen at Nana's apartment—the black-and-white tile, the heavy gold-framed mirror, the enormous vases or whatever they are, the painting I'd loved so much from the time I was a child of a mysterious, leafy glade, the old silver-dust light of Nana's past. I was always shocked into sleepiness when I saw the place, as if a little mallet had bonked me on the head, sending me far away.

Or in Connecticut, Eileen said. I looked at her. Isn't that where they drive in from? she said. He's a wonderful man, your brother. So kind and thoughtful. And his wife, too. They always know just how to cheer your grandmother up. And that's one cute little girl they've got.

How's Nana doing? I asked.

A while since you've seen her, Eileen commented.

I live on the other side of the country! I said.

I know that, dear, Eileen said. I've seen your picture. With the trees. Before the second stroke she liked me to sit with her and go over the pictures.

I stared. Nana? Bill had told me to prepare myself, but still—family souvenirs with the nurse? It's supposed to mean something to be one person rather than another.

Eileen accompanied me into the living room. Nana was dozing in one of the velvet chairs. I sneezed. Soldiers were marching silently toward us across the black-and-white desert of an old television screen. An attractively standardized smiling blond woman in a suit replaced them. Does Nana watch this? I asked. She seems to like having it on, Eileen said. I keep the sound off, though. She can't really hear it, and I'd rather not. Wake up, dear, your granddaughter's here to see you. Don't be surprised if she doesn't recognize you right off, Eileen told me. Dear, it's your granddaughter.

It's Lulu, Nana, I said, loudly. Nana surveyed me, then Eileen. Neither Bill nor I had inherited those famous blue eyes that can put holes right through you, though our father had, exactly, and so had our brother, Peter. Where does all that beauty go when someone finishes with it? If something exists how can it stop existing, I mused aloud to Jeff recently. Things take their course, Jeff said (kind of irritably, frankly). Well, what does *that* mean, really—*things take their course*? Jeff always used to be (his word) charmed that I wasn't a (his word) sucker for received (his phrase) structures of logic. Anyhow, if something exists, it exists, is what I think, but when Nana turned back to the TV she did actually look like just any sweet old lady, all shrunk into her little blanket. I bent and kissed her cheek.

She winced. It's Lulu, dear, Eileen shouted. One of Nana's hands lifted from the pale cashmere blanket across her lap in a little wave, as if there were a gnat. I'll be in the kitchen, Eileen said. Call me if you need me. I sat down near Nana on the sofa. I was not the gnat. Nana, I said, you look fabulous.

Did she hear anything at all? Well, anyhow, she'd never gone in for verbal expressions of affection. Someone sighed loudly. I looked around. The person who had sighed was me.

The last time I'd seen Nana, her hearing was perfect and she was going out all the time, looking if not still stunning, still seriously good, with the excellent clothes and hair and so on. She was older, obviously, than she had been, but that was all: older. It's too drastic to take in—a stroke! One teensy moment, total eclipse. In my opinion, all moments ought to contain uniform amounts of change: X many moments equal strictly X much increase in age equal strictly X much change. Of course, it would be better if it were X much *decrease* in age.

Oh, where on earth was Bill? Though actually, I was early. Because last week when I'd called my old friend Juliette and said I was coming to the city to see Nana, she said sure I could stay at her place and naturally I assumed I'd be hanging out there a bit when I got in from the airport and we'd catch up and so on. But when I arrived, some guy, Juliette's newish boyfriend, evidently—Wendell, I think his name might be— whom she'd sort of mentioned on the phone, turned out to be there, too. *Sure, let's just kill them, why not just kill them all,* he was shouting. Juliette was peeling an orange. I'm not saying kill *extra* people, she said. I'm just frightened; there are a lot of crazy, angry maniacs out there who want to kill us, and I'm frightened. *You're frightened,* he yelled. *No one else in the world is frightened?* Juliette raised her eyebrows at me and shrugged. The orange smelled fantastic. I was completely dehydrated from the flight because they hardly even bring you water anymore, though when I was little it was all so fun and special, with the pretty stewardesses and trays of little wrapped things, and I was just dying to tear open Juliette's fridge and see if there was another orange in there, but Wendell, if that's what his name is, was standing right in front of it shouting, *What are you saying? Are you saying we should kill everyone in the world to make sure there are no angry people left who want to* hurt *anyone?* So I waited a few minutes for him to finish up with what he wanted to get across and he didn't (and no one had ever gotten anything across to Juliette) and I just dropped that idea about the orange and said see you later and tossed my stuff under the kitchen table and plunged into the subway. When Juliette and I were at art school together, all her boyfriends had been a lot of fun, but that was five or six years ago.

Happy laundry danced across the screen on a line. Little kids ate ice cream. A handsome man pumped gasoline into a car, jauntily twirled the cap back on the gas tank, and turned to wink at me. A different standardly attractive woman in a suit appeared. It was hard to tell on this ancient black-and-white set what color we were supposed to believe her hair was. Red, maybe. She was standing on the street, and a small group of people, probably a family, was gathered around her. They were black, or anyhow not specifically white, and they were noticeably fatigued and agitated. Their breath made lovely vapor in the cold. One of them spoke distractedly into a microphone. The others jogged up and down, rubbing their arms. Someone was lying on the pavement. The possibly red-headed newscaster looked serene; she and the family appeared to have arrived at the very same corner from utterly different planets by complete coincidence. She had a pretty good job, actually. A lot better than selling vintage clothing, anyhow.

REVENGE OF THE DINOSAURS

And maybe she was getting some kind of injections. Then it was the blond newscaster again, bracketing a few seconds in which a large structure burst slowly open like a flower, spraying debris and, kind of, limbs, maybe. The blond newscaster was probably getting injections herself. I'd been noticing lines maybe trying to creep up around near my eyes, lately. But even when I was a little child I felt that people who worry about that sort of thing are petty. Of course, when I was a little child I wasn't about to be getting sneak attacks from lines anytime soon. Hi, Nana, I said, sure you're okay with this stuff? But she just kept gazing at the images supplanting each other in front of her.

One way or another it had gotten to be a few months since Bill had called to tell me about Nana's initial stroke. I'd intended to come right out to see her, but it wasn't all that easy to arrange for a free week, and Jeff and I were having sort of vaguely severe money problems, and I just didn't manage to put a trip together until Bill called again and said that this time it was really serious. I reached over and rested my hand on Nana's. Nana had pretty much looked out for us—me and Bill and Peter—when our mother got sick (well, died, really) and our father started spending all his money on cars and driving them into things. If it hadn't been for Nana, who knows what would have happened to us.

Nana gave my hand a brief, speculative look that detached it from hers, and then she turned back to the TV. From what closet had that old apparatus been unearthed? Nana had always gotten her news from the *Times*, as far as I knew, and other periodicals. I wondered what she was seeing. Was it just that the shifting black-and-white patterns engaged her attention, or did she recognize them as information and find solace in an old habit of receiving it? Or did she still

have some comprehension of what was happening in front
of her?

Enormous crowds were streaming through streets. Refu-
gees! I thought for an instant, my hands tingling. Evacuations!
But a lot of the people were carrying large placards or ban-
ners, I saw, and I realized this must be one of the protests—
there was the capitol building, and then something changed
and the Eiffel Tower was in the distance, and then there was
something that looked like Parliament, and then for a second,
a place I couldn't identify at all, and then another where there
were mostly Asians. The apartment was stifling! Despite the
horrible freezing weather I got up to open the window a
crack. When I sat down again, Nana spoke. Her voice used to
have a penetrating, rather solid sound, something like an
oboe's, but now there were a lot of new threadlike cracks in
it—it was hoarse, and strange. I suppose you have no idea how
I happen to be here, she said. This is where you live, Nana,
I said, in case she'd been speaking to me; this is your home.
Nana examined my face—dispassionately, I think would be
the exact right word. No wonder my father had been terrified
of her when he was growing up! *Thank you*, she said, apropos
of what, who could say. She folded her hands primly and
ceased to see me.

My brain rolled up into a tube and my childhood rushed
through it, swift pictures of coming here to this apartment
with my mother and father and Peter and Bill—swift-moving,
decisive Nana, smelling simply beautiful when she leaned
down to me, and her big, pretty teeth, and all the shiny, silver
hair she could twist up and pin in place in a second with
some fantastic ornament. The ornate silver tea service, the delicate slice of lemon floating and dreaming away in the fragile
cup, the velvet chairs, the painting of the mysterious, beautiful,

leafy world on the wall that you could practically just *enter* . . . the light, as soon as you opened the door, of a different time, the lovely, strange, tarnished light that had existed before I was born . . . Translucent scraps of coming to see Nana went whirling through the tube and were gone. Nana, I said.

Doll-like figures sprayed into the air, broke open and poured out blackness. There was a bulldozer, and stuff crumbling. Eileen came in. Would I like a cup of tea, she asked me. Thanks, I told her, no. She paused for a moment before she went away again, squinting at the screen. Well, who knows, she said. But I'm glad I don't have sons.

Nana had come into the world at the end of one war and lived through part of another before she left Europe, so she must have seen plenty of swarming crowds in her time and crumbling stuff and men in uniforms and little black pinpricks puncturing the clear sky and swelling right up. Jeff and I don't have a TV. Jeff doesn't like anything about TV. The way the sets look, or the sound it makes, or what it does to your brain. He says he's not so dumb that he thinks he can outsmart the brainwashing. He likes to keep his brain clean all by himself, and it does have a sparkly, pristine quality, despite the fact that it's a bit squashed by events at the moment, which occasionally causes him to make remarks that could be considered vaguely inappropriate. For example, the other day we were going up in the elevator of the office building where Jeff and his team do their research, and there was a guy standing next to us, wearing a light blue kind of churchy suit, and Jeff turned and said, sort of to him, in a low voice, It's sunset.

The guy glanced at Jeff and then at his watch. He had really nice eyes—candid, I think you'd say. He glanced at Jeff again and said, Would you mind pushing seven? Jeff said, Yup, the sun is setting, you guys at the helm. He pushed seven and turned back to the guy. See it sink toward the horizon, he said, feel the planet turn? Hear the big bones crunch at the earth's hot core? The woolly mammoths, the dinosaurs, hear that? The fossil fuels sloshing? Crunch, crunch, slosh, slosh, Dinosaur Sunset Lullaby? I nodded to the guy when he got out at seven, but he wasn't looking. Normally, Jeff is very cogent, and he's amazingly quick to spot the specious remark or spurious explanation, especially, these days, if I'm the one who's made it. I don't especially mind having a TV around myself, but my concentration isn't all that terrific in certain ways and I really can't get myself to sit down and follow what's going on in that little square window, so maybe I'm not as vulnerable to assault as Jeff is. But if someone turns a TV on in a bar, for example, I don't just have to run out screaming.

So obviously, I never actually see a TV unless we happen to go out, which we really can't spare the money to do these days, even if we were to feel like it (which Jeff certainly doesn't). But TV or not, I had no trouble recognizing those faces appearing in front of me as I sat there next to Nana. I suppose everyone knows those faces as well as if they were tattooed on the inside of one's eyelids. There they are, those guys, whether your eyes are open or shut.

Gigantic helicopters were nosing at some mountains. I felt worn out. Flying is no joke at all these days! The interrogations at the airport, and worrying about the nail scissors, and those dull boomings, even though you know it's only luggage getting vaporized, and then when you finally do get mashed into place on the clanking, rickety old thing, with your blood clotting up, and the awful artificial, recirculated whatever it is, air or whatever, who doesn't think of great chunks of charred metal falling from the sky. Oh, well. I'd gotten to Nana's in any case.

A recollection of my father and Nana sitting in this room back when they were on viable terms, drinking something from fragile, icy little shot glasses, pressed itself urgently upon me. Though of course, when Bill finally did stride in, allowing his overcoat to slip off into Eileen's hands, Peggy behind him, I was glad enough not to be sprawled out hiccuping. You beat me, Bill said, and kind of whacked me a bit on the back, that's a first. Unfair, I said, when am I ever late these days? How would I know? Bill said. You live on the other side of the country.

Peggy was carrying an enormous vase full of lilies, a funereal flower if ever there was one. Hi, Peggy, I said. Some flowers you've got there. Melinda here, too? Hi, Aunt Lulu, Melinda called from the hall, where she was studying the magical glade. I had a sudden memory of the guy who'd given Nana that painting—Mr. Berman. What a handsome old man! He was one of Nana's suitors after she booted out Dad's dad. Dad used to refer to Mr. Berman as the Great Big Jew. Mr. Berman was very nice, as I remember, and rich and handsome, but Nana was sick of getting married, so he moved on, and Nana never looked back, I think. It wasn't in her nature.

Peggy was staring at the TV. Goodness me, she said, and picked up the remote. A few sluttish teenagers flounced around a room with studio decor. That's better, Peggy said. She chuckled wanly. I calculated: the big gloomy bouquet must have cost about what I make in a week. Hey, Melinda, I said, as she wandered into the room; they brought you along, great. My sitter's mad at me, she said, they didn't have any choice. She looked at me—Alternative? Sure, I said, that's fine: they didn't have any alternative. The hell we didn't, Bill said. We could have left her on a mountain with her ankles pierced. Melinda swiveled her head toward him, then swiveled it back. Your father's just being funny, I said. You thought that was funny, Aunt Lulu? Melinda said. Cute outfit, hon, Peggy told me, fanciful; the fun shirt is what? Pucci, I said, early seventies? An as-is—there's a cigarette burn, see?

Hey, Granana, Melinda said, watchin' a show, huh. She peered at Nana scientifically and waggled her fingers in a little wave. Then she walked backward into the sofa and plopped down, showing her teeth for a moment as though she'd performed a trick. So what's going on? she asked no one in particular.

There were about five teenagers. One was a boy. They were all making faces and pausing for the silent audience to laugh, apparently. Peggy, who had a gift, rubbed Nana's hands and sort of chattered. Nana looked around and spoke in the strange voice that sounded like it had been shut away, gathering dust. Everyone, she said. Hi, Nana! we all said. Hello, Lulu, dear, she said, are you here? She blinked once, like a cat, and yawned. It was an odd sight, our elegant Nana's body and its needs taking precedence that way. She looked back at the TV, and said, What.

What the hell is this? Bill said, squinting at the flouncing, mugging teenagers. He flicked the remote, and there were those familiar guys again, standing around a podium beneath a huge flag. Bill grunted, and set the remote back on the table with a sharp little click. He forgot about the TV and started ranging around the room, absently picking up objects and turning them over, as though he was expecting to see price tags. Poor Bill. He was frowning a frown, which he'd no doubt perfected in front of his clients, that clearly referred to weighty matters. Terrible, he was muttering; terrible, terrible, terrible, terrible. His feelings for Nana were complicated, I knew (though he didn't seem to), heavily tinged with rage and resentment, like his feelings for everyone else. Our brother Peter was the quote unquote outstanding one, so Bill, as the other boy, had naturally suffered a lot growing up and was kind of arrested, being so compensatorily dutiful. He looked as if he was incredibly tired, too. Poor Nana, he said. Poor, poor, poor Nana.

Trip okay, hon? Peggy asked me. Where are you staying? One-two punch, huh, I said. You're so funny, Peggy said vaguely. You always make me laugh. She looked tired herself. Outside, someone was making some sort of commotion. Screaming or something. Bill went to the window and closed it. Listen, he said to me, thank you for coming. He had already acquired a drink, I noticed—how had he managed that? I'm glad to be here, I said; it's natural, isn't it? You don't have to thank me. Good, he said. He frowned his frown again. I'm glad you decided to come. Because decisions have to be made, and I wanted us to be united. Against? I said.

Against? he said. Decisions have to be made and I wanted you to be part of the process.

I've had a lot of practice in not getting pissed off at Bill, who can't help his patronizing, autocratic nature. I reminded myself severely (A) that he's just a poor trembling soul, trying to keep himself together in whatever way he can, that I should appreciate that it was Bill, obviously, who was dealing with Nana's whole thing here, and (B) that I wouldn't want to start regressing all over the place. Thanks, I said. Thanks for including me.

Bill nodded, I nodded.

Thanks for including me, I said again. But I don't have anything to contribute, remember?

I never *said* that, he said. I *never* said that you don't have anything to contribute. Be straightforward for a moment. Do you think you could be straightforward for a moment? That's merely the construction you chose to put on a perfectly harmless suggestion I made once—once!—that you might try just a little harder, in certain circumstances. We'll go into another room for a minute, shall we, you and I?

Melinda and I will stay right here with your nana, said Peggy, who has a sort of genius for pointless remarks. Bill and I strolled down the long hall to the dining room. I don't suppose you happen to know where the, um, liquor cabinet is, I said. What is it you require, Bill said, absinthe? There's not enough stuff right over there on the credenza? Huh? I said. He said, That's what it's called, a credenza—is that all right with you? I said, Maybe you could be a little straightforward yourself. He said, Sorry. I'm under a lot of, um . . .

Poor Bill. Obviously Dad wasn't going to be pitching in here. Or Peter, who's in Melbourne these days. Peter left the whole scene practically as soon as he could *walk*. When Peter was little everyone thought he'd be the one to find a cure for cancer, but he became sort of an importer instead, of things that are rare wherever he happens to be living, so he can be away all the time. From anywhere. Away, away. Away away away away away. Bill at least gets some satisfaction in thinking Peter's work is trivial—which really makes Jeff snicker, since Bill works for insurance companies, basically figuring out why they don't have to pay the policyholders. Now, *there's* something trivial, Jeff said. But then he said no, actually, that it wasn't trivial at all, was it, it was huge. And that Peggy was even worse than Bill, because Bill was born exploitative and venal and he can't help it, but Peggy actually *cultivates* those qualities.

I remember once, in this very apartment, overhearing Nana telling my father that he was weak and that he resorted to the weapon of the weak—violent rage—and that he used his charm to disguise the fact that he was always just about to do whatever would make everyone most miserable. I provided you with grandchildren, Dad told her. Does that make you miserable? I thought that was what every mother wanted from her child. How can you complain about your grandchildren?

How? Nana said. Peter is brilliant, but damaged. Lucille is certainly well meaning, and she isn't a ninny, despite appearances, but she's afraid of reality just like you. Only *she* expresses it in immaturity, laziness, confusion, and mental passivity.

Well, that was a long, long time ago, of course, but I still remember feeling kind of sick and how quiet it was. It was so quiet I could hear the foliage in the painting rustle and the silvery dust particles clashing together. What about Bill, my father said. Surely you don't intend to spare Bill? Even from behind the door where I was hiding, I could hear Nana sigh. Poor Bill, she said. That poor, poor Bill.

Hey, that's my brother you're talking about, I told Jeff when he criticized Bill, but the fact is, I guess I did that thing that people say people do. Which is that one quality I evidently sought out in my lover is a quality that runs in my family—the quality of having a lot of opinions about other people. Low opinions, specifically.

And Nana would have to recognize now, if she were only compos, that Bill had taken charge of her well-being all by himself, and that he was doing a pretty good job of it. Eileen, for example. Eileen seemed terrific, nothing wrong with Eileen. Listen! I said to Bill. Listen, I want to tell you this with complete sincerity: I know you've had to deal with a lot here, and I'm really, truly sorry I haven't been much help. How could you have been any help? Bill said. You live on the other side of the country.

And besides, I said.

Bill did something with his jaw that made it click. There were dust covers over the chairs. He pulled one aside and sat down. Then he got up and pulled another aside for me. When did she stop going out? I said. When did she stop going out, he said, hooking the words up like the cars of a little toy train, when did she stop going out. When she stopped being able to walk, Lucille? After her first stroke? Kind of hard to get around if you can't walk.

Well, I guess I assumed she'd use a wheelchair or something, I said. Or that someone would take her. A driver, or someone.

Anyhow, she didn't want to see anyone, he said. I told you that, I know I told you that. And more to the point I suppose, she didn't want anyone to see her.

Bill was looking stricken. The fact is, Nana was an amazing person, even if she had been pretty rough with our father, who obviously deserved it anyway. She had seen a lot in her life, she'd experienced a lot, but from all those experiences there weren't going to be many, you might say, artifacts, except for, oh, the tea service and maybe a bit of jewelry and a few pamphlets or little books, I guess, that she'd written for the institute (foundation?) she worked with. At. With. At. *The tradition of liberal humanism,* I remember Dad saying once, with hatred, as though something or other. Anyhow, there wasn't going to be much for the world to remember our shiny Nana by, except for example her small, hard, rectangular book on currency. It's incredible, I can't ever quite wrap my head around it—that each life is amazingly abundant, no matter what, and every moment of experience is so intense. But so little evidence of that exists outside the living body! Billions of intense, abundant human lives on this earth, Nana's among them, vanishing. Leaving nothing more than inscrutable little piles of commemorative trash.

I could see that Bill was suffering from those thoughts, too. I put a hand on his arm and said, She didn't want people to see her, but she let *you* see her.

Bill flushed. I don't count, he said.

As far back as I can remember, he was subject to sudden flashes of empathy that made him almost ill for a moment, after which he was sure to behave as if someone had kicked the KICK ME sign on his rear end. Anyhow, you and I have to make some decisions, he said. Like what? I said.

He gave me plenty of time to observe his expression.

Do you know how much this sort of private care costs? he said. Sure, she was well-to-do by your standards. And by mine. But you might pause to consider what will have happened to her portfolio in this last year or so. Mine will go back up in due course, yours will go back up— Portfolio? I said. But hers won't, Bill said. She doesn't have the time. In another year, if she lives, she'll be propped up over a subway grating in the freezing cold with a paper cup to collect change. So the point is that every single thing here has to be decided. And it has to be decided either by *us*, or by *me*. None of it's going to happen automatically. Honestly, Lulu— you still don't seem to get it. How do you think Nana came by her nurses? Do you think they just showed up on the doorstep one morning?

Bill rubbed the bridge of his nose as if *I* were the one having the tantrum. The point is, he said, there seems to be no chance of significant recovery. So what will happen with her things, for example? Who will go through her papers? Can we find a better place for her to be? These are decisions.

These were *not* decisions, I didn't bother to point out to Bill, who was looking really *so* pathetic with his silly jacket and premature potbelly, they were questions. This is Nana's apartment, I said. This is where she lives. We can't just, what, send her off on an ice floe.

I appreciate your horror of the sordid mechanics, Bill said. But stay on task, please, focus. I mean, driver! Good lord, Lulu. *What* driver? You know, Geoff is a fine man, I like Geoff, and it's a big relief to see you settled down, finally, with someone other than a blatant madman. But Geoff is as impractical as you are. More impractical, if possible. He takes an extreme view of things, and I know he encourages you in that as well.

I'm capable of forming my own extreme views, I said. And if you're referring to the tree painting project, it was hardly *extreme*. We all just picked one tree that was going to be deforested, and commemorated that particular tree in paint. I don't call that *extreme*.

I agree, Bill said. It's perfectly harmless. And that's great, because you have to be prudent. Courage is one thing, and simplistic rashness is another. There are lists, you know. Lists, lists, lists.

Simplistic *rashness*? I said. You know what Jeff has been doing, you know what he's been studying! I was shouting at Bill but I was thinking about poor Jeff, lying in bed this last month or so, scrawling on sheets of paper. When I'd urge him to eat, he'd start intoning statistics—how many babies born with this, how many babies born with that. I know, I said the other day, I know; don't tell *me*, tell *them*. We've *told* them, he said, that's why they cut off the funding! He did manage to write a song or two about it, at least, and he sang one on his friend Bobby Baines's 6 a.m. radio slot. You'd be surprised what Jeff can wrap a good tune around. I wish he'd get back to his music. It used to be so much fun, hanging out with his band. My mouth was still open, I noticed, and yelling at my brother. The funding's been cut off, my mouth was yelling. For the whole study! And now they're saying, Depleted uranium, wow, it's great for you, sprinkle it on your breakfast cereal! Is it any wonder Jeff isn't a barrel of laughs these days? Is it any wonder he's on a short fuse? Extreme! You're the one who's extreme! I can absolutely *hear* how you're trying to pretend his name is spelled! Jeff is *Jewish*, okay? Do you think you can handle it? His name is Jeff with a *J*, not Waspy, Waspy Geoff with a G, but every time you send us so much as a note, it's Dear Lulu and Geoff with a G!

Bill was just standing there with his arms folded. At least I send the occasional note, he said. And please don't pretend you don't know what a portfolio is. Please, please don't.

We looked at each other for a long, empty moment. The Corot will have to be sold, he said.

Sold, I said.

Well, I don't know why it should have made a difference to me. Sold, not sold—it wasn't as if I could have hung the thing up on our stained, peeling wall or whatever. But still! That word—sold! It's like inadvertently knocking over a glass!

Sold, Bill said. The jewelry's already been sold. Eek, I said. Who knew. Oops, sorry, you did, I get it, I get it, I get it, I abase myself and so on. Bill cleared his throat. Anyhow, he said.

He gestured at the cloth-draped room. Obviously, there's a lot of stuff left, but none of it's worth anything to speak of. Peggy's researched pretty thoroughly. Still, if there's anything you want, now's the time to claim it.

Now's the time. Now's the time. Who wants to hear that about anything? Thanks, I said.

Was there anything of Nana's I'd ever particularly coveted? I closed my eyes. Wow, to think that Nana had been showing Eileen that clipping of me and and my tree and my painting! Okay, so maybe the project hadn't been so effective, but at least there'd been a clipping! Had Nana been proud? Did she think I looked nice? Wait a minute, I said, Nana's still alive! You get no argument from me there, Bill said. But how much of this stuff do you think she's going to be using from now on? Do you think she'll be using the tea service, for example?

The tea service? I said. Do you want the tea service? he said. The tea service! I said. That great, big, hulking, silver thing? What on earth would I do with the tea service? How on earth do you think Jeff and I are living, out there in the woods? Calm down, Lucille, Bill said, for heaven's sake. Please don't go Dad's route.

Why on earth are we talking about the tea service? I yelled. Excuse me a minute.

I went into the kitchen, where Eileen was sitting, grabbed a glass from the cupboard, and clattered some ice cubes into it from a tray in the freezer. Excuse me, I said. Help yourself, dear, Eileen said.

There was a printed notice stuck to the door of the fridge with a magnet that looked like a cherry. Do Not Resuscitate, the notice said. Oh, shit, I said.

Eileen nodded. She's a lovely lady, your grandmother, she said, but I just kept looking at her, as though I were going to see something other than a nurse in a white uniform sitting there.

When I went back out to the dining room it appeared that Bill had gone back to the others, so I made a pit stop at the cruh-*den*-za to fill my glass and returned to the living room myself.

Anyhow, we weren't talking about the tea service, Bill said, *you* were talking about the tea service.

The tea service? Peggy said.

Want it? I said.

That's so sweet of you, hon, Peggy said.

Bill flashed an expression just like one of Dad's—pure gleeful, knowing malevolence. He'd obviously stopped by the good old credenza himself again and was gulping away at his tumbler. Eileen came in and helped Nana drink a glass of water with something in it to make it thick enough for her to swallow, and gave her a pill. A little water dribbled from the corner of Nana's mouth. Nana didn't appear to notice it. Eileen wiped it away, and then wiped at something leaking from Nana's eye. Melinda had her hands over her ears. Those *airplanes!* she said, I can't stand the sound of those *airplanes!* Why are there so many airplanes here?

Oh, don't fuss, Melinda, Peggy said, there are airports in New York City, and so naturally there are airplanes. And in any case, that's a helicopter, Bill said. Is it going to drop a bomb on us? Melinda said. Don't be silly, sweetie, Peggy said, they're not dropping bombs on us, we're dropping bombs on them.

Helicopters don't drop bombs, Melinda, Bill said, they're probably looking for someone. Who? Melinda said. The police, Bill said, hear those sirens? No, but who are the policemen looking *for*? Melinda said with her hands over her ears again. How would your mother and I know who the policemen are looking for? Bill said. Some criminal, I suppose.

Melinda flopped over, facedown onto the sofa, and let out a muffled wail. Just calm down, please, Melinda, Peggy said. You're upsetting your great-grandmother. Melinda cast a glance at Nana, who was gazing levelly at the images I'd seen earlier of the gracefully exploding building. I wondered where the building was—what country, for instance.

Things were always occurring suddenly and decisively inside the TV. Another building, for example, was just getting sheared off as we watched, from an even taller one standing next to it. Why is everyone always so mad at me? Melinda said.

I'm not mad at you, I said. Are you mad at Melinda? I asked Bill and Peggy. Of course not, Peggy said. You are, too, Melinda said. We are not *angry* with you, Peggy said. And I've told you repeatedly that when you pay for the paint job, you can put tape wherever you like.

I was doing it for you! Melinda said. I was just doing it for you! She turned to me. It said to do it, she said. It said to get tape and put plastic over the windows because of the poison, and my sitter was up in my room with her boyfriend so I got the tape from the drawer and some garbage bags, and then Stacy was mad at me, too, even though I didn't tell that she and Brett were upstairs having—

I don't want you talking like that, Peggy said. About Stacy or anyone else, young lady. Girls in real life don't behave like television floozies. I'm limiting your viewing time.

What did I *say*, what did I *say*? Melinda said and lapsed into loud, tearing wails that sounded like she was ripping up a piece of rotting fabric. Stop it, Melinda! Peggy said. Stop that right this instant—You're getting hysterical!

She's so theatrical, Peggy said to me, rolling her eyes. She put her arms around Melinda, who continued crying loudly. There's no reason to get so *excited*, Melinda, she said, you're just overtired.

Soldiers were marching across the screen again. Peggy was gazing at them absently, her chin resting on Melinda's soft hair. Was Melinda going to be a numbskull like her parents? I wondered, but then I reminded myself how much stress Peggy and Bill were under, worrying about Nana all the time, and whatever. Peggy was looking so tired and sad, just gazing droopily at the screen. She sighed. I sighed. She sighed. Do you remember when people could have veal chops whenever they wanted? she said. Bill had a yen for veal chops yesterday, so I went to the market and I practically had to take out a *mortgage*.

Are we poor? Melinda said, and hiccuped. Ask your mother, Bill said, looking like Dad again. Peggy glared at him.

I was trying to remember what Nana wrote in her little book on currency . . . *fixed, floating, imports, exports, economies* . . . And then I tried to remember what exactly had happened in the last wars we'd fought, or anyhow, in the last vaguely recent ones—just who exactly was involved, and so on. So many facts! So much new information always coming out about these things, after they've occurred. It's pretty hard to keep straight just what's been destroyed where and how many were killed. Well, I guess it's not that hard for the people who live in those places. And Jeff always has a pretty solid grasp on that stuff, and Nana sure used to . . . I wondered what she thought she was looking at now, if she thought she was actually seeing back, seeing pictures from her own life—memories, the inside of her own head . . . She seemed to be focusing on the screen so intently, as if she were concentrating on some taxing labor. Really working out what that screen was showing. Well, that was Nana! Always work work work work work. There was the sheared-off building, and the tall one still standing right next to it. I wondered what that tall building was, and I wondered what she thought it was. It looked like an office building, with black windows. Maybe Nana thought Death's office was there, behind those black windows. Maybe she pictured Death as a handsome old man in uniform, sitting at his desk and going over his charts and graphs. Behind him she'd be seeing a huge map with pins in it and his generals, with those familiar, familiar faces. He'd look tired—so much to do!—and sad. He wouldn't notice the glass tear leaking from his glass eye.

Guess we'll all be going together one of these days, Bill said. Swell, I said. You know, guys, I'm really tired. I'm going to go back downtown to Juliette's. We can talk over everything tomorrow, okay?

Do you have enough money for a taxi, Lulu? Bill said.

Do I have enough money for a taxi? Of course I have enough money for a taxi, I said. I was wishing I hadn't spent most of my last check before Jeff's funding was cut on those white Courrèges go-go boots. But discounts are about the only perk of my job, and I do have to say that the boots look pretty fabulous. Anyhow, I said, I'm going to take the subway.

The subway! Peggy said. Don't be *insane*, Lulu.

Don't die, Aunt Lulu! Melinda said.

For pity's sake, Melinda, Peggy said. No one's going to *die*.

Was I ever hoping that Wendell had finished trying to tenderize Juliette and I could just flop down on her futon! *No rest for the wicked,* Dad used to say, chortling, as he'd head out for a night on the town. (Or for the saintly, is what Jeff has to say about *that*, or for the morally indecipherable.)

Oh, look—Peggy said, pointing to the screen, where a grinning person in a white coat was standing near some glass beakers and holding what looked like a little spool—I think they must be talking about that new thread!

What new thread, what new thread? Melinda said.

That new thread, Peggy said. I read an article about this new thread that's electronic. Electronic? I think that's right.

Anyhow, they've figured out how to make some kind of thread that's able to sense your skin temperature and chemical changes and things. And they're going to be able to make clothes that can monitor your body for trouble, so that if you have conditions, like diabetes, I think, or some kind of dangerous conditions, your clothes will be able to register what's going on and protect you.

That's *great*, huh, Granana, Melinda said. She threw her little arms around Nana, who closed her eyes as if she were finally taking a break.

THE FLAW IN THE DESIGN

I float back in.

The wall brightens, dims, brightens faintly again—a calm pulse, which mine calms to match, of the pale sun's beating heart. Outside, the sky is on the move—windswept and pearly—spring is coming from a distance. In its path, scraps of city sounds waft up and away like pages torn out of a notebook. Feather pillows, deep carpet, the mirror a lake of pure light—no imprints, no traces; the room remembers no one but us. "Do we have to be careful about the time?" he says.

The voice is exceptional, rich and graceful. I turn my head to look at him. Intent, reflective, he traces my brows with his finger, and then my mouth, as if I were a photograph he's come across, mysteriously labeled in his own handwriting.

I reach for my watch from the bedside table and consider the dial—its rectitude, its innocence—then I understand the position of the hands and that, yes, rush-hour traffic will already have begun.

I pull into the driveway and turn off the ignition. Evening is descending, but inside no lights are on. The house looks unfamiliar.

It looks to me much the way it did when I saw it for the first time, years ago, before it was ours, when it was just a house the Realtor brought us to look at, all angles and sweep—flashy, and rather stark. John took to it immediately—I saw the quick alliance, his satisfaction as he ran his hand across the granite and steel. I remember, now, my faint embarrassment; I'd been taken by surprise to discover that this was what he wanted, that this was something he must have more or less been longing for.

I can just make out the shadowy figure upstairs in our bedroom. I allow myself to sit for a minute or so, then I get out of the car and close the door softly behind me.

John is at the roll-top desk, going over some papers. He might have heard me pull into the drive, or he might not have. He doesn't turn as I pause in the bedroom doorway, but he glances up when I approach to kiss him lightly on the temple. His tie is loosened; he's still in his suit. The heavy crystal tumbler is nearly full.

I turn on the desk light. "How can you see what you're doing?" I say.

I rest my hand on his shoulder and he reaches up to pat it. "Hello, sweetheart," he says. He pats my hand again, terminating, and I withdraw it. "Absolutely drowning in this stuff . . ." He rubs the bridge of his nose under his glasses frames, then directs a muzzy smile my way.

"Wouldn't it be wonderful to live in a tree," I say. "In a cave, with no receipts, no bills, no records—just no paper at all . . ." I close my eyes for a moment. Good. Eclipsed—the day has sealed up behind me. "Oh, darling—did you happen to feed Pod?"

John blinks. "No one told me."

"It's all right. I didn't expect to be so late. Maybe Oliver thought to."

Gingerly, I stroke back John's thin, pale hair. He waits rigidly. "Any news?" I ask.

"News," he says. "Nothing to speak of, really." He turns back to the desk.

"John?" I say.

"Hello, darling," he says.

"Lamb chops," Oliver observes pleasantly.

"I'm sorry, sweetie," I say. "I'm sure there's a plain pizza in the freezer, and there's some of that spinach thing left. If I had thought you'd be home tonight, I would have made something else."

"Don't I always come home, Mom?"

" 'Always'?" I smile at him. "I assumed you'd be at Katie's again tonight."

"But don't I always *actually* come home? Don't I always come home *eventually*, Mom, to you?"

He seems to want me to laugh, or to pretend to, and I do. I can't ever disguise the pleasure I take in looking at him. How did John and I ever make this particular child, I always wonder. He looks absolutely nothing like either of us, with his black eyes and wild, black hair—though he does bear some resemblance to the huge oil portrait of John's grandfather that his parents have in their hallway. John's father once joked to me, are you sure you're the mother? I remember the look on John's face then—his look of reckoning, the pure coldness, as if he were calculating his disdain for his father in orderly columns. John's father noted that look, too—with a sort of gratification, I thought—then turned to me and winked.

"You're seriously not going to have any of these?" John says.

Oliver looks at the platter.

This only started recently, after Oliver went off to school. "You don't have to, darling," I say.

"You don't know what you're missing," John says.

"Hats off, Dad." Oliver nods earnestly at his father. "Philosophically watertight."

Recently, John has developed an absent little laugh to carry him past these moments with Oliver, and it does seem to me healthier, better for both of them, if John at least appears to rise above provocation.

"But don't think I'm not grateful, Mom, Dad, for the fact that we can have this beautiful dinner, in our beautiful, architecturally unimpeachable open-plan . . . *area*. And actually, Dad, I want to say how grateful I am to you in general. Don't think, just because I express myself awkwardly and my vocabulary's kind of fucked up—"

John inclines his head, with the faint, sardonic smile of expectations met.

"—Sorry, Dad. That I'm not grateful every single day for how we're able to preside as a *family* over the things of this world, and that owing to the fantastic education you've secured for me, I'll eventually be able—I mean of course with plenty of initiative and hard work or maybe with a phone call to someone from you—to follow in your footsteps and assume my rightful place on the planet, receiving beautiful Mother Earth's bounty—her crops, her oil, her precious metals and diamonds, and to cast my long, dark shadow over—"

"Darling," I say. "All right. And when you're at home, you're expected to feed Pod. We've talked about this."

Oliver clasps my wrist. "Wow, Mom, don't you find it poignant, come to think of it? I really think there's a poignancy here in this divergence of paths. Your successful son, home for a flying visit from his glamorous institution of higher education, and Pod, the companion of your son's youth, who stayed on and turned into a dog?"

"That's why you might try to remember to feed him," I say.

Oliver flashes me a smile, then ruffles grateful Pod's fur. "Poor old Pod," he says, "hasn't anyone fed you since I went away?"

"Not when you're handling food, please, Oliver," John says.

"Sorry, Dad," Oliver says, holding up his hands like an apprehended robber. "Sorry, Mom, sorry, Pod."

And there's the radiant smile again. It's no wonder that the girls are crazy about Oliver. His phone rings day and night. There are always a few racy, high-tech types running after him, as well as the attractive, well-groomed girls, so prevalent around here, who absolutely shine with poise and self-confidence—perfect girls, who are sure of their value. And yet the girls he prefers always seem to be in a bit of disarray. Sensitive, I once commented to John. "Grubby," he said.

"Don't you want the pizza?" I say. "I checked the label *scrupulously*—I promise."

"Thanks, Mom. I'm just not really hungry, though."

"I wish you would eat something," I can't help saying.

"Oh—but listen, you guys!" Oliver says. "Isn't it sad about Uncle Bob?"

"Who?" John says. He gets up to pour himself another bourbon.

"Uncle Bob? Bob? Uncle Bob, your old friend Bob Alpers?"

"Wouldn't you rather have a glass of wine, darling?" I ask.

"No," John says.

"Was Alpers testifying today?" I ask John. "I didn't realize. Did you happen to catch any of it?"

John shrugs. "A bit. All very tedious. When did this or that memo come to his attention, was it before or after such and such a meeting, and so on."

"Poor Bob," I say. "Who can remember that sort of thing?"

"Who indeed," John says.

"We used to see so much of Uncle Bob and Aunt Caroline," Oliver says.

"That's life," John says. "Things change."

"That's a wise way to look at things, Dad." Oliver nods seriously. "It's, really, I mean . . . *wise.*"

"I'm astonished that you remember Bob Alpers," I say. "It's been a long time since he and your father worked together. It's been years."

"We never did work together," John says. "Strictly speaking."

Oliver turns to me. "That was back when Uncle Bob was in the whatsis, Mom, right? The private sector? And Dad used to consult?"

John's gaze fixes on the table as if he were just daring it to rise.

"But I guess you still do that, don't you, Dad—don't you still consult?"

"As you know. I consult. People who know something about something 'consult,' if you will. People hire people who know things about things. What are we saying here?"

"I'm just saying, poor Uncle Bob—"

"Where did this 'uncle' business come from?" John says.

"Let me give you some salad at least, darling. You'll eat some salad, won't you?" I put a healthy amount on Oliver's plate for him.

"I mean, picture the future, the near, desolate future," Oliver says. He shakes his head and trails off, then reaches over, sticks a finger absently right into a trickle of blood on the platter, and resumes. "There's Uncle Bob, wandering around in the night and fog, friendless and alone . . ."

John's expression freezes resolutely over as Oliver walks his fingers across the platter, leaving a bloody track.

"A pariah among all his former friends," Oliver continues, getting up to wash his hands. "Doors slam in his face, the faithless sycophants flee . . . How is poor Uncle Bob supposed to live? He can't get a job, he can't get a job bussing tables! And all just because of these . . . phony *allegations*." John and I reflexively look over at one another, but our glances bounce apart. "I mean, wow, Dad, you must know what it's like out there! You must be keeping up with the unemployment stats! It's *fierce*. Of course *I'll* be fine, owing to my outrageous abundance of natural merit or possibly to the general, um, esteem, Dad, in which you're held, but gee whiz, I mean, some of my ridiculous friends are worried to the point of throwing really up about what they're all going to do when they graduate, and yet their problems *pale* in comparison to Uncle *Bob's*."

"Was there some dramatic episode I missed today?" I say.

"Nothing," John says. "Nothing at all. Just nonsense."

"I just don't see that Bob could have been expected to foresee the problems," I say.

"Well, that's the *reasonable* view," John says. "But some of the regulations are pretty arcane, and if people are out to get you, they can make fairly routine practices look very bad."

"Oh, dear," I say. "What Caroline must be going through!"

"There's no way this will stick," John says. "It's just grandstanding."

"Gosh, Dad, that's great. Because I was somehow under

the impression, from the— I mean, due to the— That is, because of the—"

"Out with it, Oliver," John says. "We're all just people, here."

"—the *evidence*, I guess is what I mean, Dad, that Bob *knew* what that land was being used for. But I guess it was all, just, what did you call that, Dad? 'Standard practice,' right?"

John looks at him. "What I said was—"

"Oops, right, you said '*routine practices*,' didn't you. Sorry, that's *different*! And anyhow, you're right. How on earth could poor Bob have guessed that those silly peasants would make such a fuss, when KGS put the land to such better use than they ever had? *Beans?* I mean, *please*. Or that KGS would be so sensitive about their lousy, peasant sportsmanship and maybe overreact a bit? You know what? We should console Uncle Bob in his travails, open up our family to receive him in the warmth of our love, let him know that we feel his pain. Would Uncle Bob ever hurt a fly? He would not! Things just have a way of *happening*, don't they! And I think we should invite Uncle Bob over, for one last piece of serious *meat*, before he gets hauled off to the slammer."

John continues simply to look at Oliver, whose eyes gleam with excitement. When I reach over and touch John's hand, he speaks. "I applaud your compassion, Oliver. But no need to squander it. I very much doubt it's going to come to that."

"Really?" Oliver says. "You do? Oh, I see what you mean. That's great, Dad. You mean that if it seems like Uncle Bob might start naming names, he'll be able to retire in style, huh."

"*Ooo*kay," John says. "*All* right," and a white space cleaves through my brain as if I'd actually slapped Oliver, but in fact Oliver is turning to me with concern, and he touches my face. "What's the matter, Mom? Are you all right?"

"I'm fine, darling," I say. He reaches for my hand and holds it.

"You went all pale," he says.

"I applaud your interest in world affairs," John says. "But as the situation is far from simple, and as neither you nor I were *there* at the time, perhaps we should question, just this once—this once!—whether we actually have the right to sit in judgment. This will blow over in no time, Oliver, I'm happy to be able to promise you, and no one will be the worse for it. And should the moment arrive in which reason reasserts its check on your emotions, you will see that this spectacle is nothing more than a witch hunt."

"Well, *that's* good," Oliver says. "I mean, it's bad. Or it's good, it's bad, it's—"

"Do you think we might cross off and move on?" John says.

"Sure thing, Dad," Oliver says, dropping my hand.

John and Oliver appear to ripple briefly, and then a cottony silence drops over us. Even if I tried, I doubt I would be able to remember what we'd just been saying.

Oliver prongs some salad, and John and I watch as he lifts it slowly toward his mouth. It actually touches his lips, when he puts it down abruptly, as if he's just remembered something important. "So!" He beams at us. "What did you gentle people do today?"

John pauses, then gathers himself. "The office, naturally. Then I caught a bit of the hearings, as I have to surmise that you and Kate did."

"We did, Dad, that's very astute." Oliver nods seriously again, then turns to me with that high-watt smile. "Your turn, Mom."

"I went into town," I say. I stand up suddenly and walk

over to the fridge, balancing myself on my fingertips against the reflective steel surface, in which I appear as a smudge. "I had an urge to go to the museum." I open the fridge as if I were looking for something, let the cool settle against me for a moment, close the door, and return to the table.

"You look so pretty, Mom!" Oliver says childishly. "Isn't Mom pretty, Dad?"

"Your mother was the prettiest girl at all the schools around," John says wearily. For a moment, we all just sit there again, as if someone had turned off the current, disengaging us.

"And what about you, Oliver?" John asks. "What news?"

"None," Oliver says, spearing some salad again.

"None?" John says. "Nothing at all happened today."

Oliver rests the fork on his plate and squints into the distance. "Gosh, Dad." He turns to John, wide-eyed. "I think that's right—nothing at all! Oh, unless you count my killing spree in Katie's physics class."

"Seriously not funny," John says.

"Whoops, sorry," Oliver says, standing up and stretching. "Anyhow, don't worry, Dad—I cleaned your gun and put it nicely back in the attic."

"*Enough*," John says.

"You bet, Dad." Oliver bends down to kiss first John and then me. "I'm going upstairs now, to download some pornography. See you fine folks later."

The moon is a cold, sizzling white tonight, caustically bright. Out the window everything looks like an X-ray; the soft world of the day is nowhere to be seen.

"When did you last talk to him about seeing Molnar?"

John is sitting at the desk again. I glance at him then turn back to the window.

"He won't," I say.

"What are you looking at?" John says.

I close the blinds. "He won't see Dr. Molnar. He won't agree to see anyone. He doesn't want to take anything. He seems to be afraid it will do something to his mind." I sit down on the bed. Then I get up and sit down at the dressing table.

"Do something to his mind?" John says. "Isn't that desirable? I treat him with kid *gloves*. I'm *concerned*. But this is getting out of hand, don't you think? The raving, the grandiosity, the needling—wallow, wallow, atone, atone, avenge, avenge. And this morbid obsession with the hearings! Thank you, I do not understand what this is all about—what are we all supposed to be so tainted with? We may none of us be perfect, but one tries; one does, in my humble opinion, one's best. And explain to me, please, what the kid is doing here—what's his excuse? He should be at school."

"Darling, it's normal for a college student to want to come home from time to time."

"He's hardly 'home' in any case. For the last three days he's been with Kate every second she's not at school or asleep. I wouldn't be surprised if he actually did go to her physics class today. Why the Ericksons put up with it, I can't imagine. Have you seen that girl lately? She looks positively, what . . . *furtive*. Furtive and drained, as though she were . . . feeding some beast on the sly. What does he do to them? These wounded birds of his! It's as if he's running a hospital, providing charity transfusions to ailing vampires. That Schaeffer girl last year—my god! And before her that awful creature who liked to take razor blades to herself."

"Darling," I say. "Darling? This is a hard world for young people."

"If any human being leads an easy life, it's that boy. Attention, education, privilege—what does he lack? He lacks nothing. The whole planet was designed for his well-being."

"Well, it's stressful to be away at school. To be studying all the time and encountering so many new ideas. And all young people like to dramatize themselves."

"I didn't," John says. "And you didn't."

That's true, I realize. John took pains, in fact, to behave unexceptionably, and I was so shy I would hardly have wanted to call attention to myself with so much as a hair ribbon. I certainly didn't want drama! I wanted a life very much like the one I'd grown up with, a life like my parents'—a cozy old house on a sloping lawn, magnolias and lilacs, the sun like a benign monarch, the fragrance of a mown lawn, the pear tree a gentle torch against the blue fall sky, sleds and the children's bicycles out front, no more than that, a music box life, the chiming days.

"Young people go through things. I don't think we should allow ourselves to become alarmed. He hasn't lost his sense of humor, after all, and—"

"His—ex*cuse* me?"

"—and his grades certainly don't reflect a problem. I know you're thinking of what's best for him, I know you've benefited, but he's very afraid of medication. I don't think he should be forced to—"

"No one's forcing anyone to do anything here," John says. *"Jesus."*

"John, we don't really have a gun in the house, do we?"

"Oh for god's sake," John says. "We don't even *really* have an attic."

"Just try to be patient with him," I say. "He loves you, darling—he respects you."

"I rue the day I ever agreed to work outside of the country," John says.

"Oh, John, don't say that darling! Even when it was difficult, it was a fascinating life for us all. And Oliver was very happy."

"I *curse* the day," John says.

Strange . . . Yes, strange to think that we used to move around so much. And then we came back and settled down here, in a government town, where everyone else is always moving. Every four years, every eight years, a new population. And yet, everyone who arrives always looks just the same as the ones who left—as if it were all a giant square dance.

"What?" John says.

"How did Bob look?" I ask.

"Bob?" he says. "Older."

Driving back along the highway this afternoon, flowing along in the reflections on the windshield, the shadows of the branches—it was like being underwater. Morning, evening, from one shore to the other, the passage between them is your body.

I stroke Oliver's hair, but his jaw is clamped tightly shut and he's staring up at the ceiling, his eyes glazed with tears.

When he was little, he and I used to lie on his bed like this and often I'd read to him, or tell him stories, and he liked to pretend that he and I were characters from the stories—an enchanted prince and a fairy, the fairy who put the spell on him or the one who removes it, or Hansel and Gretel, and we would hide under the covers from whatever wicked witch.

His imagination was so vivid that sometimes I even became frightened myself.

Yesterday I was sorting through some papers upstairs at my desk, when I noticed him and Kate outside on the lawn. He was holding the lapels of her jacket and they were clearly talking, as they always seem to be, with tremendous serious-ness, as if they were explorers calculating how to survive on their last provisions. I could see Kate's round, rather sweet face—at least it's sweet when it's not flickering with doubts, worries, fears—and then Oliver held her to him, and all I could see of her was her shiny, taffy-colored hair, pinned loosely up.

It's an affecting romance. It's not likely to last long, though—none of Oliver's romances do, however intense they seem to be. Oliver is way too young. In any case, I can't help imagining a warm young woman as a daughter-in-law, some-one who would be glad for my company, rather than someone beset, as Kate always seems to be, by suspicion and resentment.

They came inside, and I could hear Oliver talking. The house was so silent I didn't have to make any effort to hear the story he was telling, a story I'd certainly never told him myself, which he must have heard from the help someplace we'd lived or stayed during our time away, a strange, winding folk tale, it seemed to be, about a man who had been granted the power to understand the language of the animals.

Oliver spoke slowly, in a searching way, as if vivid but puz-zling events were being disclosed to him one by one. Kate said not a word, and I was sure that the two of them were touch-ing in some way, lying on the sofa feet to feet, or holding hands, or clasped together, looking over one another's shoul-ders into the glimmering mist that fans out from a story. And in the long silences I could feel her uneasiness as she waited for him to find the way to proceed.

It was as if they were sleeping, making something together in their sleep—an act of memory. But I was a stranger to it, following on my own as morning after morning the poor farmer discovers the broken pots, the palm wine gone—as finally one night he waits in the dark, watching, then chases the thieving deer through the fields and hills all the way to the council of the animals—as the Leopard King, in reparations, grants him the spectacular power on condition that he never reveal it—as the farmer and his wife prosper from this power, year after year.

The story spiraled in until the farmer, now wealthy, is forced to face an enraged accuser: "I was not laughing at you," he says in desperation. "I laughed because I heard a little mouse say, *I'm so hungry—I'm going into the kitchen to steal a bit of the master's grain.*"

Oliver paused to let the story waver on its fulcrum and the shame of eavesdropping broke over me in a wave, but before I could get up and shut the door of the room or make some other alerting noise, Kate spoke. Her voice was blurred and sorrowful. "What happened then?" she said, but it was clearly less a question than a ritual acknowledgment of the impending.

"Then?" Oliver said. "So—" He seemed to awaken, and shed the memory. "—then, as all the people of the village watched, the man's lifeless body fell to the ground."

All that time we were away, during his childhood—which seems as remote to me now as the places where we were—and John was working so hard, Oliver was my companion, my darling, my *heart*. And I was shocked, I suppose, to be reminded yesterday that his childhood could not have been more different from mine, that he and I—who hardly even have to speak, often, to understand one another completely—are divided by that reality, by the differences between our earliest, most fundamental sense of the world we live in. I had never stopped to think, before, that he had heard stories from beyond the boundaries of my world. And I was really *shocked*, actually, that it was one of those stories, a story I never could have told him, that he had chosen to recount to Kate.

My gaze wanders around his pristine room, as orderly as a tribute. When he's away, no one would think of disturbing anything he has here, of course, any of his possessions. But I do sometimes come in and sit on his bed.

He's still focused at the ceiling as though he were urgently counting. "Shall I leave you alone darling?" I say. "Would you like me to leave you alone?" But he reaches for my hand.

"Oliver?" I say. "Darling?"

He blinks. His startling, long, thick eyelashes sweep down and up; his eyes glisten. "Darling, Katie is a dear girl, but sometimes I worry that she's too dependent on you. You can't be responsible for her, you know."

He draws a breath and licks his dry lips. "I can't be responsible for anything, Ma, haven't you noticed?"

"That's not true, darling. You're a very responsible person. But I just want to be sure that you and Katie are using protection."

He laughs, without lifting his head or closing his eyes, and I can tell how shallowly he's breathing. "Protection against what, Ma? Protection against Evildoers?"

"I don't want to pry, darling. I just want to set myself at ease on that score."

"Be at ease, Ma. Be very at ease. You can put down your knitting, because whatever you're fantasizing just isn't the case."

Well, I don't know. I remember, when we returned to the States, how it seemed to me, the onslaught of graphic images that are used to sell things—everywhere the perfect, shining, powerful young bodies, nearly naked, the flashing teeth, the empty, perfect, predatory faces, the threat of sexual ridicule, the spectre of sexual inadequacy if you fail to buy the critical brand of plastic wrap or insurance or macaroni and cheese. Either the images really had proliferated and coarsened during our absence or else I had temporarily lost something that had once kept the assault from affecting me.

I became accustomed to it again soon enough, though, and I don't know that I would have remembered the feeling now, that feeling of being battered and soiled, unless I'd just been reminded of Oliver's expression when, for example, we would turn on the television and that harsh, carnal laughter would erupt.

Maybe Oliver's fastidiousness, his severity, is typical of his generation. These things come in waves, and I know that many of Oliver's friends have seen older brothers and sisters badly damaged by all sorts of excesses. And it is a fact that Oliver spent his early childhood in places where there was a certain amount of hostility toward us—not us personally, of course, but toward our culture, I suppose, as it was perceived, and it wouldn't be all that remarkable, I suppose, if his view of his native country had been tarnished before he ever really came to live in it.

There were a lot of changes occurring in all the places where John had to go, and foreigners, like ourselves, from developed countries, were seen to represent those changes. Fortunately, most of the people we encountered personally received us, and the changes that accompanied us, with great enthusiasm.

In time, it came to feel to me as though we were standing in a shrinking pool of light, with shapes moving at the edges, but, especially at first, I was delighted by the kindness, the hospitality of the local officials, by parties at the embassies. Everyone was always kind to Oliver, in any case—more than kind.

And there were always children around for Oliver to play with, the children of other people who had come to help, the engineers and agronomists and contractors of various sorts and people who were conducting studies or surveys, and children of the government officials to whose parties we went and so on, who invariably spoke English. And sometimes there would be a maid on the premises, or a gardener, who had children. But when we would drive by local markets or compounds, or even fenced-off areas, Oliver would cry—he would *scream*—to play with the children he saw outside the car window.

John would explain, quietly and tirelessly, about languages, about customs, about illnesses. We brought Oliver up to share—naturally—but how does a child *share* with another child who has nothing at all? I always thought, and I still think, that John was absolutely right to be cautious, but the fact is, when Oliver was a bit older and John was away for some days, I would sometimes relent and let Oliver play with some of the children whom, for whatever reason, he found so alluring.

Oliver had spent so little time on the planet, so all those places we went were really his life—his entire life until we came back—and maybe I didn't take adequate account of that. Sometimes now, when I hear one of those names— Nigeria, or Burma, or Ecuador—any of the names of places where we spent time—it is as lustrous to me as it was before I had ever traveled. But usually what those names bring to my mind now are only the houses where we stayed, all the houses, arranged for us by the various companies John was attached to, similarly well equipped and comfortable, where I spent so much time waiting for John and working out how to bring up a child in an unfamiliar place.

Oh, there were beautiful things, of course—many beautiful and exciting things. Startling landscapes, and the almost physical thrill of encountering unaccustomed languages and unaccustomed people, their music, their clothing, their faces, the food—the sharp, dizzying flash of possibilities revealed—trips into the hectic, noisy, astonishing towns and cities.

Sometimes, on a Sunday afternoon, when he wasn't traveling around, John liked to go to a fancy hotel if there was one in our area, and have a comically lavish lunch. Or, if we were someplace where the English had had a significant presence, a tea—which was Oliver's favorite, because of the little cakes and all the different treats and the complicated silver services.

There was the most glamorous hotel, so serene, so grand. The waiters were handsome—truly glorious—all in white linen uniforms that made their skin look like satin, dark satin. And their smiles—well, those smiles made you feel that life was worth living! And of course they were charming to Oliver, they could not have been more charming.

And there were elegant, tall windows overlooking the street, with heavy, shining glass that was very effective against the heat and noise, with long, white drapes hanging at their sides. It was really bliss to stop at that hotel, such a feeling of well-being to sip your tea, watching the silent bustle of the street outside the window. And then one afternoon, beyond the heavy glass—I was just pouring John a second cup, which I remember because I upset it, saucer and all, and could never get the spot out of my lovely yellow dress—there was a sort of

explosion, and there was that dull, vast, sound of particles, uni-
fied, rising like an ocean wave, and everyone on the street was
running.

Well, we were all a bit paralyzed, apparently, transfixed in
our velvety little chairs—but immediately there was a *whoosh*,
and the faint high ringing of the drapery hardware as the
waiters rushed to draw the long, white drapes closed.

Early on, John would sometimes describe to me his vision
of the burgeoning world—lush mineral fields that lie beneath
the surface of the earth and the plenitude they could generate,
great arteries of oil that could be made to flow to every part
of the planet, immense hydroelectric dams producing cascades
of energy. A degree of upheaval was inevitable, he said, painful
adjustments were inevitable, but one had to keep firmly in
mind the long-term benefits—the inevitable increases in em-
ployment and industry, the desperately needed revenues.

Well, in practice things are never as clear, I suppose, as they
are in the abstract; things that are accomplished have to *get* accomplished in one way or another. And in fairly fluid situa-
tions, certain sorts of people will always find opportunities.
And that, of course, is bound to affect everyone involved, to
however slight a degree.

In any case, eventually there was a certain atmosphere.
And there were insinuations in the press and rumors about
the company John was working with, and it just wasn't fun for
John anymore.

It was an uncomfortable, silent ride to the airport when
we finally did come back for good. I remember Oliver staring
out the window at the shanties and the scrub and the barbed
wire as John drove. There was a low, black billowing in the sky
to one side of us, fire in the distance, whether it was just brush
or something more—crops or a village or an oil field, I really

don't know. And after we returned, there was a very bad patch for John, for all of us, though John certainly had done well enough financially. Many people had done very well.

"What is it, darling?" I ask Oliver. "Please tell me. Is one of your courses troubling you?"

He turns to gaze at me. "One of my courses?" His face is damp.

"You're not eating at all. I'm so worried about you, sweetheart."

"Ma, can't you see me? I can see you. I can see everything, Ma. Sometimes I feel like I can see through skin, through bone, through the surface of the earth. I can see cells doing their work, Ma—I can see thoughts as they form. I can hear everything, everything that's happening. Don't you hear the giant footfalls, the marauder coming, cracking the earth, shaking the roots of the giant trees? What can we do, Ma? We can't hide."

"Darling, there's nothing to be frightened of. We're not in any danger."

"His brain looks like a refinery at night, Ma. The little bolts of lightning combusting, shooting between the towers, all the lights blinking and moving . . ."

"Darling—" I smile, but my heart is pounding. "Your father loves you dearly."

"Mother!" He sits bolt upright and grabs me by the shoulders. "Mother, I've got one more minute—can't you see me, there, way off in the distance, coming apart, flailing up the hill, all the gears and levers breaking apart, falling off—flailing up the hill at the last moment, while the tight little ball of fire hisses and spits and falls toward the sea? He'll close his fist, Ma, he'll snuff it out. Are you protected by a magic cloak? The cloak of the prettiest girl at school?"

"Please, darling—" I try to disengage myself gently, and he flops back down. "Oh, God," he says.

"What, darling? Tell me. Please try to tell me so that I can understand. So that I can understand what is happening. So I can try to help you."

"It's all breaking up, Ma. How long do I have? I'm jumping from floe to floe. Do I have a minute? Do I have another minute after that? Do I have another minute after that?"

I run my hands over his face, to clear the tears and sweat. "This is a feeling, darling," I say. My heart is lodged high up near my throat, pounding, as if it's trying to exit my body. "It's just a feeling of pressure. We've all experienced something like it at one time or another. You have to remember that it's not possible for you to fix every problem in the world. Frankly, darling, no one has appointed you king of the planet." I force myself to smile.

"Every breath I take is a theft," he says.

"Oliver!" I say. "Please! Oh, darling, listen. Do you want to stay home for a while? Do you want to drop one of your courses? Tell me how to help you, sweetheart, and I will."

"It's no use, Ma. There's no way out. It was settled for me so long ago, and now here's your poor boy, his head all in pieces, just howling at the moon."

During that whole, long time, when we were away, I used to dream that I was coming home. Almost every night, for a long time, I dreamed that I was coming home. I still dream that I am coming home.

I stand, for a moment, outside the bedroom door.

"Well, there you are," John says, when I bring myself to open it. "I was calling for you. Didn't you hear me?"

"I was . . . Do we have any aspirin?"

"Come in," he says. "Why don't you come in?"

The blinds are drawn, the house is a thin shell. The acid moonlight pours down, scalding.

"Talking to your son?" he asks.

"John?" I say. "Do you remember if Oliver ever had a nurse—maybe in Africa—who told him stories?"

"A 'nurse'?" John says. "Is he having some sort of nineteenth-century European colonial hallucination?"

I sit down at the dressing table. In the mirror, I watch John pacing slowly back and forth. "He needs reassurance from you, darling," I say. "He needs your approval."

"My approval? Actually, it seems that I need *his* approval. After all, I'm an arch criminal, he must have mentioned it—he's not one to let the opportunity slip by. I'm responsible for every ill on the planet, didn't he spell it out for you? Poverty? My fault. Injustice? My fault. War somewhere? Secret prisons? Torture? My fault. Falling rate of literacy? Rising rate of infant mortality? Catastrophic climate change? New lethal viruses? My fault, whatever is wrong, whatever might some-day go wrong, whatever some nut thinks might someday go wrong, it's all my fault, did he not happen to mention that? The whole world, the future, whose fault can any of it be? Must be dear old Dad's."

I rest my head in my hands and close my eyes. When I open them again, John is looking at me in the mirror.

After a moment, he shakes his head and looks away. "I noticed we're running low on coffee," he says.

I turn around, stricken, to face him. A neat, foil packet, weighing exactly a pound—such a simple thing to have failed at! "I meant to pick some up today—I completely forgot, I'm so sorry, darling. But there's enough for you in the morning."

He looks back at me, sadly, almost pityingly, as if he had just read a dossier describing all my shortcomings. "Enough for me?" he says. "But what about you? What will you do?"

"I don't mind," I say. "It doesn't matter—it's fine. I'll get some later—I have to do a big shop tomorrow, anyhow."

"No," he says. "I'll go out now. Someplace will still be open."

John's car pulls out. The sound shrinks into a tiny dot and I feel it vanish with a little, inaudible *pop*. I listen, but I can't hear a thing from Oliver's room—no music, or sounds of movement. I'll check on him later, after John has gone to sleep. I begin to brush my hair. It's surprisingly soothing—it always has been; it's like an erasure.

It's extreme to say, "I do my best." That can never quite be true, and in my opinion it's often just a pretext for self-pity, or self-congratulation—an excuse to give yourself leeway. Still, I do *try*. I try reasonably hard to be sincerely cheerful, and to do what I can. Of course I understand Oliver's feeling—that he's lashed to the controls of some machine that eats up whatever is in its path. But this is something he'll grow out of. As John says, this is some sort of performance Oliver is putting on for himself, some melodrama. And ultimately, people learn to get on with things. At least in your personal life, your life among the people you know and live with, you try to live responsibly. And when you have occasion to observe the difficult lives that others have to bear, you try to feel gratitude for your own good fortune.

I did manage to throw out his card. I couldn't help seeing the name; the address of his office twinkled by. But I made an effort to cleanse them from my mind right away, and I think I'd succeeded by the time the card landed in the trash basket.

There's no chance that he would turn out to be the person who appeared to me this afternoon, really no chance at all. And I doubt I'm the person he was imagining, either—which for all I know, actually, was simply a demented slut. And the fact is, that while I might not be doing Oliver or John much good, I'm certainly in a position to do them both a great deal of harm.

I'd intended to stay in today, to run some errands, to get down to some paperwork myself. But there we are. The things that are hidden! I felt such a longing to go into town, to go to the museum. It's not something I often do, but it's been a difficult week, grueling, really, with Oliver here, ranging about as if he were in a cage, talking talking talking about those hearings and heaven only knows what—and I kept picturing the silent, white galleries.

Looking at a painting takes a certain composure, a certain resolve, but when you really do look at one it can be like a door swinging open, a sensation, however brief, of vaulting freedom. It's as if, for a moment, you were a different person, with different eyes and different capacities and a different history—a sensation, really, that's a lot like hope.

It was probably around eleven when I parked the car and went down into the metro. There was that awful, artificial light, like a disinfectant, and the people, silhouettes, standing and walking, the shapeless, senseless sounds. The trains pass through in gray streaks, and it's as if you've always been there and you always will be. You can sense the cameras, now, too—that's all new, I think, or relatively new—and you can even see some of them, big, empty eyes that miss nothing. You could be anywhere, anywhere at all; you could be an unknowing participant in a secret experiment. And with all those lives streaking toward you and streaking away, you feel so strongly, don't you, the singularity and the accidentalness of your own life.

We passed each other on the platform. I hadn't particularly noticed him until that second, and yet in some way he'd impressed himself so forcibly upon me it was as if I'd known him elsewhere.

I walked on for what seemed to be a long interval before I allowed myself to turn around—and he was turning, too, of course, at just the same instant. We looked at each other, and we smiled, just a little, and then I turned and went on my way again.

When I reached the end of the platform, I turned back, and he was waiting.

He was handsome, yes, and maybe that was all it was about, really. And maybe it was just that beautiful appearance of his that caused his beautiful clothing, too, his beautiful overcoat and scarf and shoes to seem, themselves, like an expression of merit, of integrity, of something attended to properly and tenderly, rather than an expression of mere vanity, for instance, or greed.

Because, there are a lot of attractive men in this world, and if one of them happens to be standing there, well, that's nice, but that's that. This is a different thing. The truth is that people's faces contain specific messages, people's faces are secret messages for certain other people. And when I saw this particular face, I thought, oh, yes—so that's it.

The sky was scudding by out the taxi window, and we hardly spoke—just phrases, streamers caught for an instant as they flashed past in the bright, tumultuous air. And no one at the reception desk looked at us knowingly or scornfully, despite the absence of luggage and the classically suspect hour. It was as solemn and grand, in its way, as a wedding.

We had taken the taxi, had stood at the desk; *we had done it*—the thought kept tumbling over me like pealing bells as we rose up in the elevator, our hands lightly clasped. And we were solemn, and so happy, or at least I was, as we entered our room, the beautiful room that we might as well have been the first people ever to see—elated as if by some solution, when just minutes before we'd been on the metro platform, clinging fiercely, as if before a decisive separation, the way lovers do in wartime.

ACKNOWLEDGMENTS

Incalculable thanks to Elizabeth Richebourg Rea and the late Michael Rea of the Dungannon Foundation, champions and connoisseurs of the short story; to Verena Nolte and the Villa Waldberta; and to the Lannan Foundation—all the people there, and in Marfa, who were so kind to me!